INTRIGUE

AT BUCKDEN TOWERS

Linda Upham

Published by New Generation Publishing in 2022

First Edition

ISBN 978-1-80369-526-6

www.newgeneration-publishing.com

New Generation Publishing

ACKNOWLEDGEMENTS

No book can be written solely by its author, and many people have helped me with various elements of the story.

I am fortunate to live in Buckden with its superb Tudor buildings, and vivid history of various occupants. The Claretian Order are generous in allowing access to the grounds, and the Friends of Buckden Towers provide interesting, guided tours.

Thank you to Sally at Buckden library, who helped me source reference books, during the covid lock-down.

Sarah Cardwell provided the Spanish translations for me – I am grateful for this help.

Graham and Lesley Bliss proof read the story and made many useful suggestions, including words for the Glossary.

Jan Clifford has again provided the wonderful illustrations – thank you.

Finally, once again, the biggest thanks go to my husband, John, for all his encouragement and determination to see the story published.

"No institution bears the monopoly of truth"

Martin Luther

The Beginning of the Story

The great road, running like a thread from north to south, wove its way through the houses and inns of the village of Bugden, providing work for many who lived here, for it was their skills which were needed to keep wagons on the road and horses shod, the drivers fed, and travellers accommodated, while the law breakers and the rogues used the same highway for less honest purposes. It was a village much like many others in Tudor England in the year of our Lord 1533.

The Tudor Dynasty's latest king – Henry VIII - has been on the throne for more than 20 years, and he is desperate to divorce his Spanish Queen Katharine of Aragon and marry Anne Boleyn.

A long, long time ago, the then Bishop of Lincoln, named Hugh, built a Palace in this village of Bugden for one reason – it was about halfway between London (where he spent most of his time at court) and Lincoln, where his Cathedral sat majestically above the town.

His successors enhanced and rebuilt the Palace, bit by bit, until its substantial Tower, walls, moat and gatehouses proclaimed that here was a rich and influential Bishop of the Church, who was powerful and secure, and who demanded subservience, as well as respect, for his exalted position in life.

And now, the latest Bishop of Lincoln (who had been the personal confessor to King Henry VIII) was providing this same Palace to his monarch, as a prison, to assist him in his drawn-out divorce from Katharine of Aragon.

The villagers of Bugden went about their humdrum daily lives in the shadow of these great brick buildings and had grown accustomed to sudden visitations by the rich and powerful of the kingdom, who came and went, quite ignorant of those whose daily work kept them in the comfort which they took for granted. Such people rarely crossed their paths, and if they did, well it was the villagers who moved out of their way – they knew their position in Tudor society.

Some Bugden residents were employed directly by the Bishop to work for him, such as his housekeeper - the widowed Mistress Fauconer, and Kitchen Agnes, who toiled endlessly in the kitchens and storerooms; others worked for him in less intimate ways like Mistress Munnings with her son Benet, whose weekly task was to wash whatever the Bishop's steward – Richard White - collected and gave to her.

As the village laundress, Charity Munnings and her son were often to be seen together within the village bounds, visiting the many inns who provided food and a place to sleep for the travellers and visitors from the road, as well as cleaning the linen for the numerous well to do families – not much escaped her eyes and ears, and she was the keeper of many secrets.

She was currently helped in her laundry by her lodger's daughter, 'Liza, who had found a home there with her mother Hannah, a skilled embroiderer; also from time to time, help was given by Ann, the wife of John Serle, Mistress Munnings' tenant.

As was usual in those times, most of the villagers were related by blood to each other, and, worked for one of the master craftsmen living in the village, or, for one or more of the landowners who lived locally.

But, however they earned their living, the majority of the men and women in Bugden were ill-educated and impoverished by the standards of the Bishop, or his Steward - several of them bordered on the destitute and in winter, their lives could easily be snuffed out.

They were all the King's subjects, but they possessed their own thoughts and ideas, which wisely in these troubled times, they kept to themselves.

Chapter 1

As Mistress Munnings, followed reluctantly by 'Liza, approached the gatehouse, one of the two new guards, who had suddenly appeared there the previous day, was picking his nose, while the other seemed to have fallen asleep standing up. The laundress could not help noticing that their green and white tunics were rather grubby and boasted several patches of varying colours. These were not the usual guards who accompanied the Bishop of Lincoln.

'Nose-picker' wiped his finger on his jerkin and sniffed, watching them from under his eyelids, then shoved his halberd forward in a menacing way, "Halt! and state your business!" he shouted at them, loudly.

"We're not deaf," replied Mistress Munnings, coldly, wincing at the volume of noise which seemed to echo around them. Nevertheless, she stopped and took a step back. 'Liza, who was following her, had halted as soon as the guard shouted at them; her small trolley was heavy with all the clean, folded linen, so she was quite glad to give her arm and shoulder a rest. 'Sleepyhead' had suddenly woken up and he too was thrusting his weapon at them in a threatening way.

"For the Lord's sake," Charity Munnings muttered under her breath, and head up, she stepped forward again. 'Liza waited patiently for the older woman to do the arguing, unsure how long this would take, or even if they would get inside the Bishop's Palace to make their delivery.

"As you can clearly see," and here the village laundress spoke slowly and loudly, pointing to her own trolley as well as to 'Liza's, "we are carrying fresh linen for His Grace the Bishop's rooms, or whoever it is that's going to be sleeping there," and she raised her eyebrows questioningly at the two men.

'Nosepicker' frowned and spat a gob of something shiny onto the ground, "None of your business old woman," he growled at her and then moved forward, raising the end of his weapon to poke at the linen, "we has orders to examine all goods, gifts and such like." He turned to his companion, "You have a look at the other one."

Charity Munnings' head came up even higher at this, and she stepped in front of the first guard, staring fiercely at the man, crossing her arms; she was not going to stand for any type of nonsense such as a search of her clean linen with a dirty pole! She was proud of her work and her reputation. Then, as she locked glances with the man, she suddenly reached out and seized the wooden shaft of the halberd firmly. There was a struggle before the guard was able to pull the weapon out of her hands.

"None of that poking my clean linen about with that filthy stick, go fetch the Bishop's steward or your sergeant or whoever is in charge of you!" she shouted at him, her voice squeaking a little with just a hint of nerves, and then pulled her trolley back out of his reach and towards 'Liza's feet.

The girl had already retreated several steps, as soon as the second guard had made as if to come towards her, as worried by the prospect of the linen being disturbed as that of her toes being run over by the trolley's heavy wooden wheels. She was not surprised in the slightest that the laundress had stood her ground with them and spoken to them so sharply, armed and unknown as they were. The laundress was well known in the village for her no-nonsense attitude and sharp tongue.

However, such flagrant disobedience by a mere woman to men placed on guard, had evidently puzzled both men who gazed at the laundress with a mixture of anger and uncertainty. Everyone stared, waiting for someone to break the sudden spell that had fallen when a voice came from behind them.

"What is happening here?" enquired a tetchy voice from within the shadows and Master White, the Bishop's Steward at the Palace appeared, his black velvet cap askew above a decidedly red and sweaty face, "tut, tut, Mistress Munnings, what is this hold up? Just when I need all the rooms finished and the helpers gone before the end of this afternoon," and he wiped his forehead with the back of his hand.

Charity Munnings merely pointed, first at her trolleys of linen and then at the guards. She raised her eyebrows.

Both guards had stepped aside immediately they heard the steward's voice (but had continued to scowl at the women) as they began their protests about following orders, and the obstructive attitude of the laundress. However, the steward told them to be quiet and berated them for keeping the women from entering the Palace when they were clearly village women, there to perform a necessary job, and unlikely to be attempting to take possession of the building! They shuffled uncomfortably and their scowls deepened even further as the steward ordered them to let both women pass immediately, now and in the future, for they were clearly no threat to anyone, and neither were their clean sheets.

The laundress bestowed a triumphant smile on the men, who pretended not to notice her, and proceeded immediately through the archway with 'Liza following just behind, head down, trying to disguise her grin. She could feel the guards' eyes boring into her back as she passed them. All through both the outer and inner courtyard Mistress Munnings tried to wheedle information out of the Steward as to why the linen was needed so quickly but with no success. He left them in the inner courtyard and the two of them carried the piles of clean linen directly into the Tower storeroom. They then stepped across into the kitchen area.

By the time Mistress Fauconer, the palace housekeeper had shared a pot of small ale with them, they knew precisely the reason for the rushed cleaning of the Tower the previous day, as well as for the sudden demand for extra, clean laundry – also for the unexpected appearance of those strange guards. The person coming to reside in the Tower at Bugden Palace was not the Bishop of Lincoln, nor was it a churchman, or even a nobleman; it was no less a person than Katharine, rightful Queen of England!

Mind you, the housekeeper had added, the Steward had given them all very strict instructions that, were they to meet her, they must address her as 'Your Royal Highness' not as Your Majesty, for she was now the Princess Dowager and no longer Henry's Queen. The title of Queen of England, was now held by another.

"You cannot have two 'Her Majesties'," added the housekeeper, at which she tossed her head and rolled her eyes to show what she thought about that particular instruction.

Mistress Munnings, understandably agog with this exciting and unexpected news, paused in the outer courtyard on her way back home, thrusting the handle of her newly emptied trolley at 'Liza, as she ordered the girl to get herself home as fast as she could and get on with the dirty laundry, piled up on the wash square in the garden.

Charity Munnings was heading into the village at high speed with this piece of twattle; however, the laundress added, pulling at her arm and stopping her for a moment, she was allowed to inform her mother of the momentous news.

‘Liza nodded. Her mother, Hannah, rarely left the laundry house, where she worked throughout the day at her embroidery orders, “She will be interested in this news seeing as how she and the Queen are both Spanish,” continued the laundress, then recollecting that ‘Liza was wasting valuable time, Mistress Munnings gave her a little push and told her to get on and get herself home.

She watched the girl set off and then scurried behind her through the outer gateway, sweeping past the two guards with her head held high and turning left into the village, made for the village pump where there was always a long queue of women, who made the ideal audience. She thought about all the friends to whom she would pay a fleeting visit along the way, thus ensuring that the whole village would know in plenty of time that a Queen was coming to live in Bugden.

Chapter 2

'Liza walked slowly into the garden, trundling the two empty trolleys behind her, but with her head buzzing with the knowledge that the Queen of England, Katharine, was coming to the Palace. She left the empty trolleys by the shed and proceeded to the wash square where the wash tubs were already full and waiting for the next stage of the cleaning process.

Her mother would be sewing in the outhut - the overhang at the back of the house - where the light was especially good, but she paused momentarily and watched as Benet Munnings twisted the water out of one of the just-washed sheets, his small, strong arms moving quickly. He was rather short sighted so he did not see her, and she managed to duck under the canopy so that she could speak alone with her mother for a few precious minutes.

Looking up at her daughter as she sidled up to her, a smile on her face, Hannah motioned for the girl to sit down next to her and carefully pushed her needle safely into the padded top of her needle case. She smiled fondly at her saying, "Well Aliza, I can see you have something of great importance to tell me."

Only her mother ever used her full name, insisting on it as a mark of respect to her dead father, who had chosen it personally. 'Liza answered to both names but was secretly pleased that her mother was the only one who called her Aliza for, it seemed to her to have created a special bond between them.

She dropped down onto the nearest stool and regaled her mother with a word-for-word account of what had just occurred at the Bishop's Palace, leaving herself breathless, such was the speed with which she completed the story.

Hannah gently pushed some of her daughter's dark, wavy hair back behind her ears and pulled her linen cap down more firmly onto her head, while she digested this information; but 'Liza brushed her hand away impatiently, "Did you hear me, Mami - the Queen of England!"

Hannah gave a brief smile, "I heard you, Aliza. I am somewhat surprised that the King should send her here. The news of him asking for a divorce so he can marry again despite it being against the Church's teaching has been known for some time. The balladeers at the inns have been singing about it all these past weeks," she paused, "I suppose that seeing the Bishop is a close friend of his, that this Palace seemed ideal,"her voice trailed off as 'Liza rudely interrupted her.

"But Mami, just think, the Queen of England here!"

Hannah looked into the garden while she framed her answer, "Why not? It is a long, long way from London and far away from those who support her cause and not the King's. I know that there have been rumours that the Spanish Ambassador hoped to bring her out of the country. Well, it is truly a very long way to any port from here!"

Hannah paused for a moment, giving the matter some more thought but then simply smiled warmly at her daughter, "Don't forget, those stories in London were about her being a woman of great resolve and determination as well as great pride; and on his last visit, Edward told us of her steadfast refusal to contemplate a divorce. She is of course completely right to do so," Hannah gave a sigh and played with some of the threads lying on her lap.

'Liza waited quietly, and Hannah continued, "She is a mother devoted to her daughter, so I doubt she would do anything that would leave her beloved Princess Mary behind to face the wrath of her father or place her position as heir to the throne in jeopardy. However, I cannot understand that bringing her here will change anything at all, for she will have to obey the King eventually; for he is both her husband and monarch."

‘Liza lifted her head back slightly and tilted it to one side while several thoughts raced across her mind; but she waited until her mother picked up her sewing frame, before repeating some of the gossip she had heard, in and around the inns, “He wants to divorce his wife, because he has no son, but why blame his wife for that?” then added, “Anyway, why shouldn’t the Princess Mary rule as Queen?”

She looked intently at her mother, “You‘ve told me often enough that Spain had a Queen as ruler, who was every bit as clever and ruthless as any man, so why is it not all right for England to have a Queen to rule them?”

Her mother looked back at her, pressing her lips tightly together before replying, “Well, Queen Isabella certainly was a very strong ruler in Spain, and determined to wage crusade for the Catholic faith.”

She sighed “But it was a difficult time for many, like my parents, your grandparents; and so many people died during all those battles, and others forced to leave Spain.”

There was a pause, as Hannah thought back to her childhood; then she shook her head to free it from those dark memories, and continued, “They do say that when Queen Katharine was growing up in Granada, she took the pomegranate as her personal emblem to remind her of the fruit trees growing in the Alhambra, in which she went to live, after the last King of the Moors was defeated.”

'Liza shrugged with one of her 'so what' expressions on her face. Her Abuelos, her grandparents, had once been a thriving part of the Jewish convert community in Spain until their persecution by Queen Isabella - the mother of this Queen Katharine. They had been forced to leave Spain but had told their granddaughter all about this wonderful Moorish palace: the ornate gardens and fountains and lacey stonework had left indelible memories on the old woman, and to amuse her granddaughter, she often drew the intricate patterns that had been gouged into the marble walls and doorways.

Hannah gently touched her daughter's arm, "I bear this Queen Katharine no ill-will, for it was her mother, Isabella, not she, who, forced my beloved parents to leave Spain, to their everlasting sorrow - and with only what they could carry on their backs." She shook her head at the sad memory.

'Liza nodded as her mother continued, "You can have no idea what they went through 'Liza, forced to sell their beautiful home, and their business for nothing, and leave all their friends, simply because the Inquisitors' suspicions were aroused against them by jealousy. Imagine how you would feel if you were made penniless and forced out of your own country, simply on suspicion of not being a true Catholic. Your Abuelos never forgave Queen Isabella for the treatment that they and their fellow Jews suffered."

"But Mami," 'Liza shook her head at her mother, knowing the truth was actually far more uncomfortable, "it was because many of the marranos really were untrustworthy," she protested.

The story of the forced exile of thousands of converted Spanish Jewish families, was one she had heard many, many times, with as many differing interpretations and embellishments each time, depending on who was doing the talking, for not all of their London friends had come from the Spanish community.

She dropped her voice adding, "And you know, it is true that Abuelita was never really a true Christian was she, I mean..." and she pointed back towards the family shofar - the ram's horn that had been lovingly preserved by her mother. She stopped as her mother frowned at her, shaking her head fiercely.

"Never ever talk about her like that; yes, your grandmother was forced to pretend to be a devout Catholic, but she was just like so many others living in Spain; she paid her obligatory dues to the Church, but I cannot deny that she did so probably to survive."

It was a very good reason, but not a good excuse and Hannah knew it, but she could never bring herself to criticise her own mother, and she bowed her head, saying softly, "In her heart, no, no, I believe she never fully forswore her own faith."

There was silence and Hannah gazed into the garden, where Benet was now filling several buckets from the well, before murmuring, "That didn't mean she was a bad person; all people do what they must to survive, Aliza, and your Abuelos were no different from hundreds of others."

"She baptised you into the Catholic faith!"

"Yes, of course I was baptised, and later, so were you. She hoped Antwerp and London were going to be safe places to live once more, but would never take a risk again, when living in any Christian country. You know that the Jewish people have often been falsely accused of all manner of evil things, so even in our home in London, in Cheapside, living among our countrymen, she could never truly trust everyone who said they were our friends."

'Liza nodded at this; among the several nationals living in and around the famous area of Cheapside, there were frequent arguments and fights, murders and vendettas as well as feasts and festivities when, after any drinking session, hot words tumbled out before cool minds had properly engaged with them.

No one liked to admit it either, but it became apparent that there were spies living within the community, for they all knew of men and women who had been suddenly arrested and taken away. You never who knew who might be listening to your conversation, and of course, with the houses so close to each other and the yards open to all, anyone could overhear you. She sucked her bottom lip in, remembering those frightening scenes when soldiers went marching in and then out of houses, with men and women bound and restrained among them, children running and crying at their side.

Her mother looked at her, and murmured, "Just so," before returning to her sewing, carefully selecting another thread for her needle. "It is a sad fact Aliza, that one people can oppress another simply because they do not share the same beliefs. Even when those same people live hard-working, law-abiding lives."

She gave a tiny sniff, "But that is the way of the world. Best not to talk about our past openly though, even here and even now." Her mother looked so terribly sad, that 'Liza suddenly leaned forward and gave her a brief hug.

Looking out into the garden, 'Liza watched Benet pouring clean water into one of the large tubs, and stood up, "I was told to get on with the laundry and help Benet; Mistress Patience at the Lion told me this morning that they had been warned to expect several guests, so she sent over an extra pile of sheets to be washed, and of course, now we know why." She stood up and dropped a kiss on her mother's head, noticing for the first time how many grey hairs were appearing amongst the black ones.

"Here," her mother reached down beside her and held out some nightgowns and a separate pile of fur edges "I have removed the tippets from these. They will need some hard work to get them clean, tell Benet best use the Hippocras. The nightshirts can go in with the rest."

Chapter 3

Benet had indeed been busy, getting the tubs ready for the washing, but he was now sitting on the grass, waiting for 'Liza or his mother, whoever should come first. He had a black and white kitten on his lap, one of a half-dozen, that the kitchen cat had birthed in the small barn. He loved kittens, tickling and stroking them until they were desperate to scramble off his lap, and he never minded when they nipped him with their sharp teeth or scratched him with their tiny claws.

'Liza kicked off her shoes and stockings, cursing at the tie on her right leg, which insisted on remaining in a knot. Finally, she bundled up her outer petticoat and shift, tucking both firmly under her belt and stepped up and into the first bucktub. She felt the black slime of the lye soap squidge coldly through her toes as she trod up and down and round and round on the sheets, the rushes separating the several layers turning soft and malleable as she stamped on them. She sighed.

Seeing her at work, Benet reluctantly got to his feet, letting the kitten drop onto the ground, where it scampered off at once, back to its mother in the barn. Plunging his arms into another tub nearby, he began his first lot of wringing out before dropping the sheet into the next tub of clean water and then picking up the next soapy, wet sheet. He gave her a grin.

'Liza nodded at him and returned to the mind-numbing job in hand. As always, she let her mind drift somewhere else, shutting out the warm afternoon around her, the sounds of the chickens clucking around the garden and the pigs snuffling and grunting. A blackbird's trill reminded her of one of her grandmother's songs, sung to her when she was small, and it began to run through her head. She found herself keeping time to that silent song, only stopping suddenly as she became aware that Benet had stopped working and was watching her.

"You get on with your job, Benet Munnings and I'll get on with mine," she told him sharply and regretted it at once, as his face crumpled, and his head drooped. He turned away and began to stretch a clean sheet into the drying rack.

"Your mother will be here soon," she called out to him, anxious to restore his good humour, "and we have news of why there has been so much work at the Palace. It's not the Bishop coming at all," she waited for him to turn back and then told him who was coming.

"T-t-t-t - today? The Q-q-q-q Queen of England?" Benet's stutter was always more pronounced when he was excited or emotional.

'Liza nodded then looked at the grey water in her tub, "Yes. Today, according to Mistress Fauconer, and poor Kitchen Agnes has had to suddenly make twice as many loaves; hurry up and finish with that sheet, I need help to tip this water away and refill the tub," and she gave him one of her bright smiles and watched his face beam back at her in response.

It often puzzled her how he could stay so happy and content as almost a man, and yet remain with the mind of a child. She was very fond of him and always did her best to save him from the cruel taunts of those villagers, like the Shelleys, who called him 'M-m-m-m moonman' imitating his stutter which grew more pronounced, of course, the more upset he became, until thoroughly frustrated he would start to cry; and that only made things worse for him and encouraged his tormentors to increase their bullying.

Benet reminded her of some of the dwarf players, the tumblers and singers, who had strolled through Cheapside from time to time, singing and music making as they went. Some of them had been acrobats too, and sometimes were accompanied by dogs or ponies; and a few times, she had seen a bear in a cage. They were always brightly dressed and certainly seemed to have extremely loud voices, despite being small and misshapen, like Benet.

After changing the water and carrying on with the familiar routine of rinsing the sheets in another tub by giving them a good stir with the wash bat, she called to Benet for help in wringing out the worst of the water, before dropping that linen in yet another tub near the wooden twisting frames, before finally hauling her used tub to the ditch at the side of the garden to be emptied. It was hot work and her arms ached by the time she helped him to spread all the wrung-out shifts across the lavender bushes which grew on the far side of the grass patch.

It was past Sext and they both looked forward to a break; small ale and hunk of bread, or perhaps a jumble or two. Hannah had made several of the twisted honey biscuits the previous day, and both 'Liza and Benet were very fond of them. Perhaps too, there would be a little time to sit and chat about the news of the Queen and when she would arrive, and how many people would come with her, and if the King would come as well.

Almost immediately, Charity Munnings swept round the corner of the laundry house, her arms full of more dirty linen, which she quickly dropped onto the stone wash square near the largest tubs. She looked around at all the linen drying on the bushes, nodding her approval before moving quickly to the rosemary bushes, where a few of the shifts and stockings had worked free from their stones and were flapping in the wind. She tutted under her breath and looked around for her workers.

Her son was sitting on his stool under the outhut, eating his third jumble, while Hannah stitched quietly behind him. There was no sign of 'Liza.

"'Liza, 'Liza, where are you? Come and deal with the vicar's linen." She called loudly and beckoned impatiently as 'Liza sidled reluctantly over to the wash square, "Hurry up and get a tub and put this lot in; it seems that the vicar has had a little problem with his food, recently," and she pursed her lips as she thrust the bundle at the girl. 'Liza wrinkled her nose at the smell, but it was nothing unusual to have to deal with dirty undergarments, it just meant it took longer to get them properly clean.

Meanwhile, the laundress pulled out another roll of linen which she had been carrying under her arm, tipping it into one of the small tubs which they used for the smallest linen pieces. "Fetch the sorrel water, Benet," she called out to her son, who hastily stuffed the last of the biscuit into his mouth as he slid off his stool, "these cuffs need a long soak if I am to get rid of the ink stains," and she unrolled each cuff as she spoke.

Charity Munnings' eagle eyes had also noticed that the nearest wooden frame, where a sheet was being stretched to dry, had a corner knob which was crooked, and so had not screwed down flat and she shook her head. "I'll have to get our Thomas to come and fix that again, it's worked loose. Mind you, he'll not mind coming here after he's finished his day's work," and she gave a sly smile as she raised her eyebrows at 'Liza, just as the sound of people cheering and shouting began to drift into the garden.

They all stopped whatever they were doing and listened carefully to the noise. "That must be her! That's the Queen coming," Charity Munnings spoke for all of them, "quickly all of you, we must see Her Majesty arrive and show her our respect!"

They all ran to the roadside at the front of the house, where the noise was noticeably louder and could see that already a group of horsemen had reached the outer gatehouse and were dismounting. They edged further towards the gatehouse and looked south, down the road which ended in London and where more riders could be seen, a large cloud of dust was rolling up behind them.

These were well-dressed gentlemen and two churchmen of some kind, followed by several ladies who were riding in one large group. Some of them were riding oddly 'Liza noticed – they were facing to the right – which Hannah told her later was a sign that they must be Spanish and not English ladies, who always rode their side-saddles to the left. The Queen was not conspicuous among these women and no crown was visible on any head either; it was only after 'Liza actually met Queen Katharine, that she realised how tiny she was and that she would have been almost invisible, riding, surrounded by her ladies, even if she had been wearing a crown!

Still, visible or not, the villagers made sure that wherever the Queen was amongst the throng of visitors, she could hear how much they supported her and valued her, for their cheers and hat throwing went on long after the whole party had entered the Tower courtyard and only the many supply wagons were left to navigate their way up the street and past the few villagers of Bugden, who found that their cheering had brought on a terrible thirst.

Chapter 4

It was only to be expected that things would become quiet again, after the tumultuous day of the Queen's arrival. Village life resumed its predictable routine; the travellers came and went up and down the great road linking London with the northern parts of the country. Gossip continued about what the removal to the Bishop's Palace meant for the Queen – and therefore the village – fuelled by much ale and beer, and encouraged by curious guests at the various inns.

Privately, Hannah hoped that the Queen would have a quiet stay at the Palace and regain some sort of settled existence, to help her cope with the stress of the much-mooted divorce proceedings and the loss of her position at court.

Nevertheless, it had come at a disturbing time for the whole country. Various stories and rumours were brought daily from London by those who stayed at one or other of the inns; no one seemed sure if war might be declared, if Queen Katharine's nephew, the Holy Roman Emperor, who sided with his aunt would avenge the insults she had been suffering, not to mention the diplomatic pressures building up thanks to King Henry's unwillingness to wait for His Holiness the Pope to give his verdict.

The Bishop of Lincoln, whose own cousin, Thomas Longland, lived in one of the large houses in the village, found himself in the strange position of having to defend the King's actions, and the role of the Church in allowing the King to re-marry without Papal authority, despite having a living wife!

Reverend White at the village church, cousin of the Bishop's steward (and to whom he owed his living at Bugden) tried hard to avoid any mention of marriage or Papal authority on doctrinal issues when composing his sermons, and ignored awkward questions or pointed arguments.

The villagers felt very strongly that Queen Katharine had been wronged, and, equally shocked that the new Archbishop of Canterbury had not adhered to canon law. What was to happen to the country if neither the King nor the Archbishop no longer obeyed the Pope and the teachings of Holy Mother Church?

The Archbishop's ruling that the King's marriage was invalid, despite no word from the Pope, undermined the whole authority of the English Church, giving cause to all sorts of doubts, and the villagers felt uneasy as their secure world wobbled; if a King could defy God's representative on earth, others might think they could defy the King or his servants and ignore his law, and then what would happen to them all?

A few husbands had wondered, aloud, if the Archbishop of the English Church was able to declare this long Royal marriage illegal, whether there might be room for more ordinary marriages to be set aside; that is until they went to bed and their wives reminded them that such a ruling would cost them more money than they had ever seen in their lives, and there were more immediate things that they should be worrying about, like the price of food and whether or not their taxes would increase.

The morning after their visit to the Palace, to return the clean laundry, Mistress Munnings received an important visitor – Steward White, who wanted to inform her that the Queen had brought her personal laundress with her, so all her own intimate needs would be met, however, he had added, there would be an increase in the amount of general laundry to be regularly cleaned now that more people were staying at the Palace, and most of them were used to having fresh linen daily.

An increase in the general laundry meant more money for her and was an unforeseen bonus for Charity, but one that she was careful not to boast about when talking to her friends and acquaintances. What it also meant was a great deal more work for 'Liza, Benet and Ann Serle, who helped out from time to time. She lived in the tiny cottage at the far end of the Munnings' property, with four young children and husband John.

Goodwife Sabey (who helped the laundress with laying out the dead) kept an eye on the young Serle children when Ann was asked to help with the laundering work or any other domestic jobs that needed doing, for the family were very poor and Ann took whatever work she could.

John Serle was not completely landless, but his strip in Westfield was a poor one and never gave him enough for his family to live on, so that he was forced to accept any job he could, and acted as odd-job man for several widows, or was tasked with taking others' teams of oxen to the fields; this was a job that suited him well, for he had a fine singing voice and could often be heard singing to the oxen as they plodded to whichever field was to be harrowed or ploughed.

It was a mean, poor life and three of their children had died before reaching their first birthdays. Ann already looked much older than Hannah, despite being many years younger, and was perpetually tired with the daily struggle to earn enough to eat and look after her family.

'Liza was determined that she would never marry a poor man and die an old woman before she was twenty and, most important of all, she never wanted to go hungry. Tonight, here, supper would be the remains of the braised hares that they had cooked the previous day. It did not do to keep meat or fish too long in the heat of summer, for the pantry, although shaded and cooler than the house, did not keep food from spoiling.

They ate well, for they could afford to buy flour from Simon Fox at the mill on the hill, and Benet managed to find time most evenings after work, to go off with some of the village boys, who allowed him to join them on their so-called hunting trips and despite his clumsiness, shared whatever bounty they had. These were quite successful, especially in the summer months when game and fish were both plentiful and the extra daylight allowed them to set their traps or fish well into the evening.

Occasionally Benet got left behind, especially when one of the landowners or his stewards went on the prowl for just such adventurers as these, and surprised them, forcing the boys to disappear quickly into the countryside, usually leaving Benet in their wake. Benet never told on them though, and he could appear to be very stupid when he wanted. It helped that few people thought he could do anything on his own initiative, so he was usually sent home with a cuff around his head and told not to trespass again, but of course he and the others took no notice of this.

One time, after he had returned home with torn clothes and a bruised cheek, 'Liza had asked the laundress why she let Benet go off with the village lads, if they did not look after him, and Mistress Munnings explained that she struggled hard not to be over-protective of him, but it was difficult for her, not least because, of course, Benet was eager to be just like any other village boy, and thus got himself involved in all sorts of japes. At least he was usually with his cousin, Thomas Gilbert, who as apprentice to his father, William, knew all the village families very well, including those who could be trusted or not. Thomas was quite tall and strong too and well able to protect Benet against any bullying if he saw it happening.

The bigger problem though, was that Thomas was determined to make 'Liza accept him as her sweetheart, and he made no attempt to hide this fact during any of the frequent family get-togethers to which Hannah and 'Liza were invited with Charity and Benet. Thomas's sister, Alice Gilbert was about the same age as 'Liza and although the two girls got on very well, Alice often tried to persuade 'Liza to agree to accept her brother, which ended in a big row, with one or the other storming off. For 'Liza, Thomas's attentions were becoming more and more embarrassing.

Many times, at night, when in bed and talking with her mother Hannah, 'Liza reiterated her decision not to marry if she could not marry a wealthy man. She preferred to talk quietly about their previous life in London, partly to hold on to the memories which seemed to slip further away with each day spent in the village.

Her mother chose to remind her on their good fortune living in a room rented from the laundress. It had not seemed so at first, even to her, she told 'Liza, for their small house in Cheapside had been so much grander, but they would never have been able to stay there after the sweating sickness killed Johannes, her husband, and then Grandmother. For a while, Hannah had been quietly desperate.

Despite her skill as an embroideress, she could not earn enough for the rent and food all by herself, and 'Liza had then been too young and small to earn money. The move here had been a hidden kindness by Mistress Reynolds, the London embroiderer who had befriended the family when they had first come to London.

In Bugden, she had said encouragingly, they would have a room to themselves, and there would always be enough food, and they would never worry about going hungry. Hannah often reminded 'Liza of the number of burials that Mistress Munnings attended throughout the year, especially in the winters when many in the village went hungry and were forced to beg what they could. The poor and hungry were the first to succumb to any illness.

They were not to know, that for her part, Mistress Munnings had very swiftly decided that Hannah and her daughter were decent people, and she was happy to have an association with them, in particular, she approved of Hannah who was well skilled at her embroidery work, so had been careful to say nothing but good of them both in the village. Her high opinion of them had been helped in no small part by their immediate acceptance of Benet - despite all his shortcomings.

He very quickly told his mother that he liked them both, not least because on their second day there, 'Liza had rescued his favourite kitten from a water-filled ditch that ran the length of the garden, getting herself thoroughly wet and filthy as a result, but earning Benet's undying loyalty.

Mistress Munnings found 'Liza strong and willing to learn the laundering work and that meant that she received an extra pair of helping hands for no money at all – a very satisfactory outcome. They never realised that by receiving the laundress's approbation, the villagers had accepted them with little resentment or suspicion, even when Hannah's Spanish past became widely known.

For Hannah and 'Liza, it had not been easy being incomers into the village; and they had taken a long time to get used to the quiet, as well as the country ways of the village, which despite being on the Great Road North from London, and busy most of the day with riders and coaches, carts and wagons, was nothing like the teeming streets of London.

Despite their acceptance by most people, simply because they lived with Mistress Munnings, 'Liza in particular, always felt slightly strange and not quite at home. She liked many things about the village and most of the people who lived there, with whom she was on good terms, and she did not even mind the work involved in helping to launder the linens (except when she had to break the ice on the tubs on a winter morning); no, it went deeper than that.

She always wondered if she would feel more settled and at home in the bustling streets of London, noisy and smelly though they were, if she ever returned. However, she soon realised that she would probably never have the chance to find out. Every time she raised the subject of leaving Bugden and returning to the city, her mother would shake her head sadly and say that they would have so much less there than they had here if they went back to their house in Old Jewry near the Mercer's Hall.

Chapter 5

Back in Bugden Palace, the Queen and her ladies and all her other servants had spent a busy two days unloading and distributing all her belongings and possessions within the Tower rooms and chapel, as well as those rooms allocated to her staff in various locations within the Palace buildings. There was a bit of grumbling about the poor, small rooms allocated to the ladies and their maids, especially from some who should have known better! It was not Her Majesty's fault, they were reminded several times by Lady Darrell, the Queen's chief Lady in Waiting.

The Queen's own horse was not with her either, for she had been expressly forbidden to ride out from the Palace, or even think of going hunting in the Bishop's extensive deer park,which lay on the far northern side of the great road and well away from the Palace and its many eyes. The grooms, who had accompanied her from her previous home at Ampthill, had been lodged above the stable and thus found themselves alongside some of the guards who had been sent there to 'protect' the Queen – leading to quite a few fights and rather a lot of pushing and shoving whenever they passed each other. It would be fair to say that there was little love lost between the two sides.

The grooms looked about them and set about re-ordering the stables and the few horses there, with the excuse that the stables were not fit for purpose for royalty, but really, as a way of irritating the guards, who were forced to help move straw and feed and tackle and help to erect more stalls.

Meanwhile, on the first floor of the Tower, which looked out at the village above the moat, the Bishop's personal rooms had been converted to an inner (bed) chamber, where the queen insisted on sleeping on her own mattress, which was sumptuously soft with its down and feather filling, and using her personal monogrammed linen and favourite bed hangings. If she could not act like a Queen in the day, she would, she told her ladies, sleep like one at night!

The outer chamber was for other daytime activities or receiving guests, if any were brave enough to come to pay court to her. Here were hung her personal tapestries, their vibrant scenes of Hercules' labours and Jason's adventures giving some life and colour to the drab walls. A small prie-dieu for Her Majesty's personal prayers, was moved several times until finding a final resting place under the small window looking out onto the small park which stretched north and west, away from the Palace buildings.

Bella, the Queen's young Moorish maid had been kept very busy all morning, but finally was able to lay the precious vellum-bound primer on the top of the prie-dieu and give the ornate silver clasps one last rub with the soft cloth she was using to wipe everything free from the dust of the road.

She had already unwrapped and stored the Queen's books, and now turned to her ivory chess set – placing the pieces as they had last been set out when they were at Ampthill. She wanted them to look as they had before they were packed away, hoping to make this new move as stress-free as possible for the Queen. She replicated their last remembered positions and held the red king and white queen in opposing hands for a few seconds. It was called the Game of Kings, but she thought 'Game of Kings and Queens' was more appropriate, given the attack and counterattack that was practised not only between the chess pieces, but between the real-life King and Queen of England. In her mind, she had named the red king 'Henry' and the white queen 'Katharine'. She sighed heavily as she placed them opposing each other on the board.

Lady Darrell had put out the wonderful gilt candlesticks on one of the exquisitely embroidered table runners, but Bella was forced to move them to one side, to accommodate the Queen's knife and spoon, to which she gave one last polish. She left the rich, gold crucifix in its box so that the Queen could place it where she wished.

The chandelier was also still in its box, as no one was sure if the ceiling was strong enough to hold its weight, although it certainly looked as if it would. Master White, the Steward, was unwilling to allow it to be hung anywhere, which made them all fearful that this was because he knew that the King would move them on again very soon.

Lady Darrell looked at the girl fondly as she swept into the chamber with a stone vase filled with freshly picked flowers. The Queen was still at prayers in the chapel, she informed Bella, but she had ordered everything to be quite ready before she came back into the room. For once, the unmissable routine of daily services augmented by frequent periods of prayer and contemplation, had given the servants a chance to complete all their jobs in both chambers.

"Bella, don't forget to wind up the clock," Lady Darrell reminded the girl, as she left the room, and Isabella duly retrieved the clock from its housing in what appeared to be a bejewelled and enamelled book, and carefully wound it. Of all the Queen's possessions, this was the one she coveted the most for herself.

However, Bella reflected, as her gaze swept around the room, nothing Her Majesty now owned was half as fine as some of the furnishings of the various royal palaces which the Queen used to call her home. Even her dresses and outer wear had started to look shabby, and there was no money allocated for new clothes. Her jewels had already been given back, by order of the King.

When the whole bitter divorce business began, Bella had feared that with each successive move and each reduction of staff, her own position would be lost and she would be dismissed with nothing and nowhere to go, but her godmother, the Queen, had constantly assured her that she would always have a home with her.

Sitting down on one of the hard chairs, Bella carefully arranged her full skirts, smoothing the nap down, and reflected not only on her good fortune in having this position as maid to the Queen, but also on her boredom. Stifled by the same routine of most days, and forced to spend her youth among older women, who, shut away from normal life indulged in petty squabbles and childish spite, she longed for a friend of her own age, someone to giggle with or share some gossip. She had suffered more than her fair share of teasing and not so light-hearted banter from the servants at every place where they had been forced to live, and it was getting wearisome.

Some of the servants could be over friendly though, and after one casual grope from a courtier, she had fled, sobbing into the Queen's bedroom where Lady Darrell had found her. Such groping was common she was told, especially on the younger maids, and the men and boys expected to get away with such unwelcome handling; it was very unlikely that anyone would do much about it if there was a complaint.

However, Lady Darrell whispered, she had found that when she had been a young girl at court, carrying a small pair of sharp snips on her girdle meant that she could inflict some well-deserved pain if she had to do so. It had been sound advice and her reputation as someone who put up a fight, now kept her safe - most of the time.

Having made a tour of the Tower and its adjoining buildings and grounds, the Queen decreed that each fine day, in the afternoon, rather than sit in the gloomy outer room in the Tower, she and her ladies would sit in the cloistered garth, near the Hall, where the fresh air and the sunshine would lift their spirits. They would sew and talk amongst themselves, listening to a life of one of the saints, usually read by the Queen. Sometimes one of the ladies played the lute but there was no longer any dancing, and no one felt like singing.

Today, the Queen wanted to discuss when and how to start her weekly alms giving; a duty she took very seriously, and now made more pressing by the need to show her appreciation to the many villagers, who had been bringing presents of one kind or another for her, ever since she arrived. The fact that most of the presents were damaged as a result of the guards' over-zealous investigating or went missing, if they happened to be particularly valuable, was merely an inconvenience that had to be suffered. None of them was in any doubt that the King was trying to drive the Queen into abandoning her firm opposition to the divorce and make her enter a convent. Each move they had been forced to make had seen a tightening of the restrictions placed on them all, and a greater degree of vigilance exercised over all they did or all they met.

For Bella, the monotony of life was depressing her usual upbeat spirits and even the consolation of her prayers did nothing to help. She would have to make her confession about her bad temper and wish to be in another household, before mass tonight, and hoped Father Abell would be kind to her.

Chapter 6

The summer weather became hotter and increasingly sultry, but the daily laundry routine continued as it always had to, but now with increased amounts to wash and scrub; at least the hot weather and strong sunshine meant that the sheets and shifts dried very quickly, and the workers could normally head for some shade over Sext – midday, and the hottest time.

Today had begun very early for 'Liza, tasked with the return of a laundry order to the village's dairywoman. Mistress Munnings had a lot on her mind, and she gabbled through morning prayers before issuing instructions to the youngsters, including the return of Goodwife Attwood's clean linen.

'Liza stepped into the cool, dim interior of the dairy, her nose wrinkling at the sour smell of curds, and placed her basket on the stone-flagged floor; she wiped her warm forehead with the back of her hand

and sighed before looking around, then caught sight of her friend Rebecca, near the back window, already red in the face with effort, as she turned the handle of one of the butter churns.

Rebecca noticed her at the same time and flashed a quick smile before raising her eyebrows and calling to someone over her shoulder, but she didn't pause, in fact if anything she speeded up the rate at which she was working. 'Liza correctly interpreted this as a warning that Rebecca could not stop to have a chat.

Goodwife Attwood, the owner of the village dairy, came into view, carrying a pile of dirty linen in her arms. She nodded at Liza, "Ah, good, it being Wednesday, I thought you'd be coming to collect this," and she dropped her pile of dirty linen on the floor.

'Liza knew what was expected of a young girl in the presence of someone older and more important, and bobbed a small curtsey, "Good morrow Goodwife Attwood," she said politely and bending down, scooped out the clean, pressed linen that the laundress had placed in her basket earlier, and left it on the nearest scrubbed table, "I have the clean linen ready here, and Mistress Munnings has asked for a crock of butter and a small cheese, if you please," and she bobbed another small curtsey.

The dairywoman's narrow lips, tightened even further at this request, but she nodded and turned to the shelves behind her, collecting the food which 'Liza put carefully in the bottom of the now empty basket, before piling all the dirty washing on top. She smiled and murmured a thank you, before risking a quick glance at Rebecca, hoping that she might be able to talk to her now the business was finished, but the glance had been noticed.

"Have you finished all the churning Rebecca?" came the sharp question.

Rebecca shook her head and grimaced at 'Liza, knowing that a gossip with her friend was now quite out of the question; the hint had been taken. Two buckets of sheep's milk were standing by the door, and 'Liza almost sent them flying as she hastened to make her escape into the fresh air.

Taking a deep lungful, she looked north up the Great London Road to see what was making such a noise. It was one of the many travelling goose-men with his flock, making their way to one of the markets in the south. His two dogs were barking loudly at the stragglers foraging at the side of the road, as they all made their slow way into the village, all contributing to a noisy background of honking and shouting and yapping.

Although only a couple of hours after sunrise, the air was very warm and 'Liza expected that the man's stop at the Tap or the Crown, would be longer than usual. In any case, the herder would have to wait for sufficient tar to soften in the tar shed, to cope with this large flock. Most geese were reshod with sand and tar here and she wondered as she always did, whether the warm tarry sand hurt the geese's feet much, as they were forced through the sticky mixture. Better a few moments discomfort than walking miles on torn webs all the way to market, wherever that was, she guessed.

Benet had been sent to all the inns just after dawn, to empty their piss pots into the big barrel. She hoped he would have already moved the barrel from out of the cart and not waited for her to help him. The smell was so acrid when it was new, but especially so in this hot weather. It made her eyes water whenever she had to use it, remaining pungent until the liquid was several days' old. Decanting the stale urine to bleach the sheets or shifts was one of her least favourite jobs, but she was grateful she did not have to regularly remove the urine in the piss pots from all the village inns and thus was spared all the ribald comments and lewd suggestions from the men in the yards, not to mention the likelihood of spilling some of the urine onto her feet or clothes.

The basket was heavy, and she set it down just short of the laundry house, her ears burning with the bad language filling the air, as two heavily laden wagons inched past each other, impatient to be moving again after waiting for the geese to clear the road; neither was prepared to give way, but at the same time, both were trying to avoid the deep potholes that stretched across the width of the road.

Further along, she could see the new guards lounging in front of the outer gatehouse. They looked like they were dozing in the warmth but, as it would soon be too hot to stand in the sun, they would disappear into the shade of the building behind them. They took no notice of either the wagons or her.

Rolling her shoulders to ease the ache in them, she picked up the basket and walked on. A dray loaded with yerms, ready for thatching, was parked at the front gate, its horse slowly chomping at the verge, so she was expecting to see the village thatcher as she turned the corner of the cottage. Yes, Tom the thatcher was on the wash square, looking up at the roof where his apprentice had just replaced a stultch, which Mistress Munnings had asked to be reset.

Tom ignored the girl as he watched his apprentice descend the ladder and 'Liza was forced to skirt around him, carrying the dairy's dirty linen to the wash square. Several tubs were ready to be used, which meant that Benet was already back – although, as usual, he was nowhere to be seen.

Dropping the linen on the ground, she detoured into the stone larder attached to the back of the kitchen near to the outhut, where the butter and cheese would stay relatively cool, and then returned to her job, sorting the pile of dirty linen and placing it near the bucktubs.

Tom Bowyer, the village thatcher was gathering his tools as Charity Munnings appeared from the back of the pig pen, where she had been disposing of the peelings and waste of the kitchen. She called out that she was just coming to pay him and hastened along, her long apron flapping around her legs. Benjamin, his apprentice, now safely on the ground, hefted the ladder onto his shoulders and stood silently. "All tight now?" she asked. Tom nodded.

"Thank you, and you too, Toad," she said to the young man, and handed Tom some coins, "This is the reckoning for this and the repair to the barn roof a while back."

He shoved these into his pocket without counting; everyone trusted the laundress to be straight and honest in her dealings. After a quick doff of his cap, Tom directed his apprentice to get to the cart, and followed him around the side of the cottage, while the laundress looked up at her roof and nodded with satisfaction at a job well done. She nodded absent-mindedly at 'Liza, on being told that the cheese and butter were in the larder, then told her to get on with the washing.

'Poor Benjamin,' thought 'Liza as she trampled the linen clean; Toad was such a cruel nickname to have, and puzzling too until she had learned that it was the custom that all thatchers' apprentices were known as 'Toad', owing to the amount of time they spent in the shallow water, keeping the rushes and sedges growing straight or replanting the roots. It was not a nice name and was somehow worse for Benjamin who, like real toads had a skin that was both spotty and rather sallow.

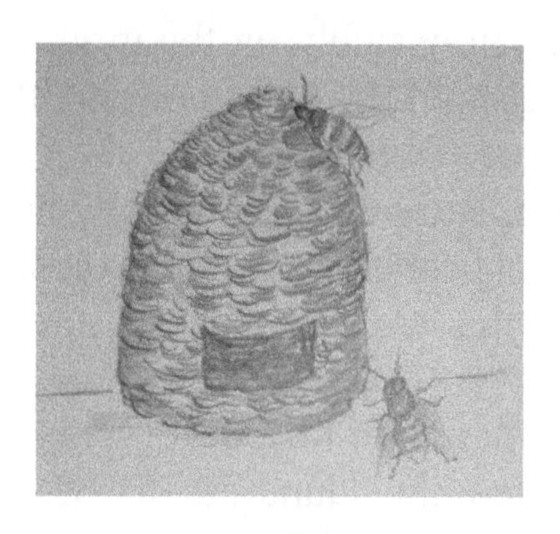

Chapter 7

In spite of no sighting of the Queen in and around the Palace, Mistress Fauconer the housekeeper was full of titbits of news when she came across with her piles of grubby linen. It seemed that some of the English ladies-in-waiting continued to moan and grumble about their removal to this remote building, and some of the Queen's maids had been quite unkind to Kitchen Agnes. Also, there was a black maid who seemed to be a favourite of the Queen, who smiled a lot but appeared to be quite shy and said very little, leading Charity Munnings to observe that she probably didn't speak much English.

'Liza could overhear most of this conversation as she pounded the shirt cuffs of Master John Gilbertson, whose family inhabited the Bugden Britten manor house opposite the church and who considered themselves far superior to all, even to the Bishop's brother who lived nearby. Mistress

Gilbertson was well known for being mean, and the proof lay in 'Liza's hands, as she endeavoured to clean the poorly woven linen with her slipstone, without damaging the surface, for the cuffs were already fraying and she had to be extra careful not to damage them further, or she would get the blame and that would mean a beating or even worse in Charity Munnings' eyes, Mistress Gilbertson would see this as a way to renege on paying her bill.

"Mind you," Mistress Fauconer was continuing with her tale, "I told them, I did, that they ought to consider themselves lucky. We might be on the edge of the Fens but this here palace is snug and warm, and we are a long way away from any prying eyes, although there are a few of those in the Palace, and we've had one or two strangers turn up here," and she took a sip from her ale pot.

"Oh?" the laundress's comment was an invitation to say more.

"Aye, we had two Friars earlier on, who come asking to see the Queen and they had hardly gone into the Chamber to see her, when another man, smart and full of himself, appears asking for Steward White. He made a point of telling me he had been sent here by the Bishop, to do some survey or other, but he seemed more than keen to find out about those Friars. I took a dislike to him there and then, and I told him, I did, that Father Abell had taken them both into the Chapel or the Chamber to meet the Queen, I couldn't remember which, and," she paused for effect, "that I was no busybody to pry into other folks' business!"

She nodded, pleased at the memory, and took another swig of ale, "I was soundly told off then for calling her the Queen, so I replied that it was difficult for a poor woman like me to remember when I had so much else to think about!"

"Oh, famously said, Ann," Charity Munnings laughed, "I must remember that!" she looked at her friend, and leaned forward slightly, "As to that well-dressed man you met, I hear from Patience Jakins at the Lion that he arrived same day as the Queen and booked himself their best room! Busy he was too, asking questions and buying drinks for all there. He seemed to be more interested in who was there and why, as getting ready to do any work."

The two women nodded in full agreement with each other, before Ann Fauconer continued, "Wouldn't surprise me if there was more to him than just being a surveyor or whatever he says he is; I mean, what would the Bishop be wanting with a survey? Master White keeps everything up to date and all the rents were paid up on time this last quarter day. Seems to me that there's a lot of unnecessary interest in what goes on in our Palace, now the Queen has come."

She gave a hearty belch and then finished the last of her ale. 'Liza could have told them that Alice Gilbert had seen the two Friars they had just mentioned being hustled into a cart by some of the guards that very morning. Alice had seen them just after sunrise as she was walking down the road towards Thomas Haynes the basket maker, having been sent to collect two new skeps for Goodwife Baxter, the bee-keeper's mother. The friars looked most unhappy, and their habits were bedraggled like they had spent the night sleeping somewhere rough.

However, she kept that to herself, the two gossips would hear of it soon enough, and she had work to get on with, in fact 'Liza had only just finished spreading some of the cleaned shifts over the far rosemary bushes when Mistress Munnings called her over. Benet and his mother were arguing loudly, and Benet looked stubborn and was scowling.

"'Liza!" Charity Munnings shouted across to her, "move yourself, I haven't got all day."

"Now, take these to Mistress Collier, she's over at the Flacks' place in Hogsherd", and she thrust several swaddling bands at the girl. "At this rate the babe will be full grown by the time she gets them," and she cuffed Benet across the head. "As for you, you lazy boy, anyone would think I asked you to walk to London the way you carried on, and if you think you're going fishing now, you can think again," and she cuffed him once more. Benet began to cry.

She turned back to 'Liza, "Then take the ones underneath to Bridge House. Nicholas Burberry has a fine new son, William, and he's doing well by all accounts. Named after his wealthy uncle for the usual reason, I'm sure." She nodded at the girl and told her to be off.

'Liza skipped out of the way, anxious not to be caught up any further in the laundress's ill humour. She had these tricky days sometimes and 'Liza had suffered many times from both tongue lashing and head cuffing, so it was best to stay out of arm's reach. She placed the thinner swaddling bands to hand, on top of the better-quality ones already in the basket and tried to think who the village midwife was attending, but Hogsherd Close housed the poorer labourers and their families, who lived alongside the enclosure for the pigs, owned by those without a garden.

Here, Thomas Attwood looked after the swine, driving them into the woods in Autumn for pannage and generally seeing to them the rest of the year, but he was a rude and rough man and she rarely spoke to him. Even his sister-in-law at the dairy avoided him as much as she could.

Strolling past the goose hut behind the smithy, busy shoeing yet more geese, she smiled at Rowland Langland and his son Michael, hard at work at the anvil, with two dray horses waiting patiently to be shod. She felt as though she was hot enough to explode, so what it must be like in the smithy next to the hot coals, she could not begin to imagine.

She delivered the swaddling bands as instructed to Patience Collier, the village midwife, whom she found sitting outside the door of one of the small, tumbledown cottages in Hogsherd. She was drinking ale from a large stone jar, and whisps of her greasy hair hung limply down the side of her face, while inside, 'Liza could hear someone moaning softly.

Seeing her look of surprise, Mistress Collier waved a hand airily, saying, "She's a way to go yet; thank Charity for me and tell her she was right. She's a proper slummock this one." She shook her head and took another swig of ale.

'Liza bobbed a curtsey and then took her time returning to the heart of the village. Outside the Lion, several carters were taking a break and among them was the man that the women had been talking about earlier. He was moving around, tankard in hand and she saw him summon Jane, the serving girl, who came forward with the ale jug to refill the tankards of the men he was talking with. Whatever or whoever the man was, he seemed to be in no hurry get on with the survey he was supposed to be doing, and the drinkers were not complaining, even though it was not even mid-morning!

She made her way to the Burberry household, where the basket was taken from her by a harassed looking Nicholas who had just arrived at his own front door; he asked her to convey his thanks to Mistress Munnings. She gave her best curtsey and said that she would convey his gratitude – she thought that sounded grand enough for an important village freeman, who was also one of the churchwardens, also it wouldn't hurt to have him think well of her.

Chapter 8

Saturday was a quiet day for village laundry, and 'Liza and Hannah used the free time to clean their own room, which lay at the back of the Munnings' house, before tackling some of their own laundry. The top sheet was turned for a second week, and the blankets hung outside to air. While her mother shook the hay-filled mattress and smoothed out any lumps, her daughter tightened the ropes slung underneath it which always sagged loose by the end of the week; then the girl took both their pillows and having beaten them well with a wooden paddle, left them in the sun too. Hannah took their shifts and aprons out to the washing square to wash them while 'Liza carefully swept their room out.

It was always difficult to keep the bare clay floor clean and free from bits of straw and hay and whatever else their shoes brought in. Hannah never liked the idea of rushes on the floor – too many lice and fleas for her taste. She spoke wistfully about the marble floors of her mother's home and how much easier they were to keep clean.

Next, 'Liza turned her attention to the hall floor and the other two rooms that opened out from there. Benet's room she always left to last. It was at the front of the house and always dark and rather smelly. 'Liza rolled up the oiled cloth hanging over the window (which Benet left down permanently) and used her apron to waft fresh air in. His bed was a mess but even she could see that the mattress cover had split, and half the hay had now fallen out onto the clay beneath and spread around the room. Sighing, she dragged the mattress into the hall, through the kitchen and out into the sunlight at the back, so that Mistress Munnings and her mother could mend it and restuff it with some more jags of hay. She picked up a broom to sweep the floor.

Hard at work on their various tasks, they were surprised to hear their names being called and to see the familiar figure of their regular London visitor, Edward Swarthye, come around the side of the house and into the garden.

Edward was Spanish, a Moor who, many years before had set up a workshop in Cheapside near the Guild of Broderers, and consequently, also close to Hannah's home shortly after her family had settled there from Antwerp. He had brought over from Toledo his specialist knowledge of steel needle making, and as no one else seemed able to find out the secret of how he made these vital pieces of equipment, he continued to make a good living in London.

She had once asked him if he preferred to live in London rather than Spain, and he had looked at her for a long time before replying, “I miss the warm sunshine, but I feel safer here; although we Moors had been accepted in Spain for many years, it did become a bit uncomfortable for us during the Reconquista by Queen Isabella.”

‘Liza nodded sympathetically, and he shrugged his shoulders, and continued, “When the last Moorish kingdom fell; there was a lot of,” he paused, considering his words, “exuberant rejoicing by the Spanish, and having seen that, I decided to move away.” He did not explain further.

He had been a regular visitor to their London home before the death of ‘Liza’s grandmother and later, her father, and she had been amazed that Edward had continued to work throughout that summer in London, ignoring the ravages of the disease and seemingly impervious to its danger.

His friend and very good customer, Mistress Reynolds, had worked for several clergymen, including the Bishop of Lincoln. There was a continual demand for the elaborately embroidered copes that were worn for the various services, and other, sumptuous gold embroidered overtunics, for a different one was needed for each of the major festivals. There were altar cloths and baptismal cloths and several other necessary pieces of linen requiring a skilful hand. When the Bishop of Lincoln had admired the gold embroidery, Mistress Reynolds had told him about Hannah and that she was happy to fulfil other similar commissions; he had been a good patron, for he had then recommended Hannah's embroidery work to his Prebend at Lincoln Cathedral.

Oliver Curren, the Prebend, whose brother was then the vicar at Bugden, was a fussy man and reluctant to travel to London especially once the sweating sickness began; he had suggested to Mistress Reynolds that Hannah leave London and come to live in Bugden for a time and work for him and other prelates and had already tasked his brother with finding suitable accommodation for her and her daughter. This turned out to be the lodging with Charity Munnings.

Oliver Curren's brother was no longer vicar of the village, but the commissions still came regularly to her. Even so, Hannah might never have come north if the sweating sickness had not killed both her mother and her husband.

While grieving for her losses, Hannah realised that the subsequent reduction of income, coupled with her fear for the health of herself and her daughter, made the offer to leave London more and more promising and, in the end, she had not needed that much persuading by Mistress Reynolds, to take up the Prebend's offer.

Having to leave Cheapside was the biggest concern however, for its position in the heart of the trading community with its easy access to everything she needed, caused her to worry that she might no longer be able to buy all the things she needed for her skilled trade, and she had confided this worry to Edward.

The needle-maker was something of a wheeler-dealer in the expatriate community and had no hesitation in promising to visit her each quarter with fresh needles, silks and threads, in fact with anything she felt she needed, assuring her that once the local families saw how beautiful her work was and how fine her Spanish black thread work, she would have more than enough commissions to give her a healthy income. It had sounded like a good idea, but over the last twelve months, the work had reduced and reduced, and Hannah was now facing the prospect of being unable to pay her rent.

It was true that Edward never failed them. Long ago 'Liza's Abuelita had haggled with him, over 'el mayor precio', his best price, and he had always enjoyed verbally sparring with her; she seemed to amuse him for he often visited their London house, just to gossip or speak Spanish and drink a glass of wine; and even now, Hannah benefited still from this pricing scheme.

However, he had not been due to visit them until the following month, which puzzled her. London was an expensive three or more days' journey from them for him, so after all the greetings and pleasantries, and

Mistress Munnings had taken her leave to look at dinner, 'Liza watched her mother and the needle-maker carefully.

He placed his large parcel of goods, wrapped in linen bindings on the seat between them, before embarking on a long, and rapid conversation in Spanish with Hannah, of which 'Liza could only hear and understand a part.

She had learned Castilian Spanish from her grandmother but over time and since her Abuelita's death, she had forgotten a lot of it, for it was something she rarely practised; her mother insisted that they speak in English at all times, so nobody could accuse them of anything suspicious like plotting against the government - a lasting worry from their time in Spain.

The only thing 'Liza had left to remind her of her Abuelita, was the book that her grandmother had made many years before in Cordoba – filled with her own designs and with an accompanying explanation of the reason they were in there – a legend or a mythical creature, a native flower or stylised picture of a monument; or simply a memory of something in her life. It was beautifully bound in soft leather with the damascene work for which her grandfather was famous. He had had it made especially for his wife and so the book was doubly precious to the girl.

She realised however, that these two seemed to be talking in some colloquial Spanish of which she knew almost nothing and even more curiously, there were some odd pauses when Edward finished speaking, and her mother looked at him intently before Edward began again. If she had not known differently, 'Liza would have suspected that Edward was trying to persuade her mother about something, and she hoped that it was not some kind of courtship.

Eventually her mother sent her to fetch some more ale for Edward and a beaker of water for herself, which meant that, reluctantly, 'Liza was forced to leave them alone. She looked back once to see them, heads down, in earnest conversation again.

Edward thanked her for his ale and smiled, telling her she was quite a young lady now, and he had brought her a gift, and from his tunic pocket he produced a bunch of red and yellow and bright green silk ribbons.

The ribbons were indeed lovely, and she knew how expensive silk was, so she thanked him in Spanish, which made him smile. Something told her not to enquire about his unexpected visit, but she watched his face for any reaction when she told him of the arrival of Queen Katharine earlier that week. His face gave nothing away though as, steepling his fingers together, he listened to her attentively before giving her a brief smile and thanking her for her vivid description of the event.

They asked him about the preparations that had been made in London, for the coronation of the King's new wife, Anne Boleyn, now named Queen, and what she was like. His description was extensive, but he finished by telling them of his surprise at the silence of the crowds as she rode by them, there were even a few boos as she passed the regilded Eleanor Cross. She had ridden gracefully and had beautiful flashing black eyes he told them, finer than his own! She rode well but must have found it uncomfortable because she was obviously pregnant.

This was a surprise to both mother and daughter, and they said so.

Edward nodded at them, "Of course, that may be partly why Henry has moved Queen Katharine ever further from London and her friends, although I am told that it was at the request of his new Queen, who bears real ill will to her predecessor. It is all a part of the drive to get her to agree to go into a convent. All my friends are outraged at the King's Proclamation last week that his marriage to Her Majesty is illegal, for it has been dissolved by his new Archbishop of Canterbury. It is a disgrace. How can an Archbishop ignore the authority of the Holy Father? It is a terrible thing to have done."

An uncomfortable silence followed this statement. 'Liza saw her mother bite her bottom lip and nod her head in agreement.

"Tell me something about how things go in London for Mistress Reynolds and her family?" Hannah asked, partly to break the silence and partly from genuine curiosity, and he responded with tales of her and their former neighbours, until interrupted by Charity Munnings, who came bustling out of her kitchen, a small brown pot in her hands. This she handed to Edward, advising him that it was a pot of her best damson jam that he had liked so much last time he had visited them.

Edward rose to his feet and bowing to her, he took both her hands to his lips and kissed them, thanking her for her kindness towards him.

'Liza watched the laundress turn bright pink, and become quite flustered at such courtly attention, before whisking herself away back into the kitchen while Edward watched her go with a smile on his face, before collecting himself and saying that John the Carrier would be waiting for him to begin his journey south again. He bade them farewell, taking Hannah's hands in both of his and asked her to think well of him and remember all he had told her.

Hannah did not reply but smiled at him, and 'Liza thanked him again for her ribbons; before both walked with him to the edge of the roadway, waving one last time as he made his way to the Tap Inn down the street.

All the while, 'Liza puzzled over why he had come to see them now and what it was that he wanted Hannah to think about. Yes, they had new needles and in the large packet, they found many coloured threads and silks, a small roll of black velvet and a small bag of pearls. Even at Grandmother's 'best price', it was an expensive bundle of goods, and yet she had seen no money change hands, neither had she been sent to their room to fetch the pouch of coins kept hidden behind the coffer. She began to wonder if Edward was indeed courting her mother.

Looking north up the road, which was empty, then south towards the village, 'Liza gave a big sigh and tucked her arm through her mother's. Hannah's brow was furrowed, and she had compressed her lips tightly together. "I can feel your thoughts buzzing round and round, but now is not the time to talk, so contain your impatience 'Liza and we will walk and talk this afternoon," her mother told her.

Chapter 9

Benet was shuffling his feet, scuffing at the stone floor as he waited for his release from church. Having finished his sneezing fit – a regular occurrence when the incense burner was swung anywhere near him – he wiped his nose on his sleeve and looked up at his mother to see if she had noticed. She had, but by then the vicar was well into the service and through the Eleisons, and, having frowned at him she carried on with her own devotions. Benet had hoped that the Queen might come to the Sunday service, wearing her crown, if possible, but she obviously remained ensconced at the Palace and must have gone to the Chapel there. He was very disappointed.

Beside him, 'Liza was mouthing the responses and the words expected of her, but her mind was busy analysing all that her mother had told her the previous evening after supper about the real reason for Edward's visit. Dutifully she began "Pater Noster," jogging Benet's arm to join in, as he was again gazing up at the roof, lost in the wonder of the brightly coloured angels on the roof above him, and who looked just like angels should look (in his opinion). He recited the service mechanically as she did as she returned to her thoughts.

Edward's vociferous support for Katharine had been a total surprise to both her and Hannah, for he had never seemed to be particularly proud of his

Spanish heritage; but for whatever reason, and because of whomever had been speaking to him – and Hannah had speculated that she thought that it might be some of the Spaniards who had come with The Ambassador, something had sparked his national pride in the Royal Spanish Princess who had married the King of England and become Queen but had been ruthlessly discarded.

Certainly, he was well placed to both hear and indulge in gossip in the many London households he served. A well-known and popular figure, he was counted a friend by high and low-born alike. Now, someone he knew had persuaded him to enlist the help of Hannah to act as a go between for the Queen and her supporters, who wished to communicate with the Queen without the King's Chief of Spies, Thomas Cromwell, or one his spies knowing about it. Probably, Hannah had said, it was for the Spanish Ambassador himself.

These messages would be secreted inside embroidered linen collars which Hannah would send on a regular basis to Edward. However, he had been unable to suggest how she would be able to see the Queen for long enough to exchange any messages, given that she was so closely watched. He had made a few suggestions but left the detail to Hannah; it was dangerous but well paid, and it was the money that had persuaded Hannah to agree.

'Liza went over all of this again and again, but try as she might, she could not see how her mother would be able to have access to the Queen of England, or be able to pass any messages under the noses of the guards or be in really close contact with anyone else who served the Queen, for that matter.

She moved her beads correctly as they all intoned the Ave Maria and realised that after the Credo and the sermon, the service would be at an end, and she would be free for a few hours. She ought to go and visit Alice, her best friend, safe in the knowledge that Thomas would be going to the Butts behind the forge, taking Benet with him; for Benet had to practise his archery along with all other able-bodied men and youth, and his uncle William, Thomas' father, had made him an especially small but powerful bow, with arrows to match.

Thomas was again a subject she needed to discuss with his sister, for his attentions towards her were causing her a great deal of embarrassment, with Mistress Munnings making comments and wondering aloud about the best time to marry. Alice though, would have her head full of her impending move to Hinchingbrooke Priory, for she had decided to begin a new life as a novice there.

Religion did not interest 'Liza in the slightest - attending church every Sunday and on the obligatory feast days was bad enough for her, so getting up for Matins just after midnight, and attending all the other services throughout the day did not appeal at all. Besides, she remembered only too well all the stories of persecution in Spain, in the name of God.

Her feet had gone to sleep so she shifted a little and risked a glance at the vicar. Whenever she looked up, he seemed to be looking straight at her as if he could read her mind, which would be very embarrassing at the moment, as she had been puzzling over what kind of intrigue would allow her mother to establish a treasonous connection with the Queen.

Service over, the villagers streamed out of the church and into the graveyard, talking loudly over the ringing of the church bells. Hannah waited patiently for Charity Munnings as she shared some morsel of gossip with old Goodwife Sabey – who helped her both with the laying out of the dead and looking after the Serle children for Ann.

Charity Munnings took the responsibility of attending to those who had died, very seriously, aided by her work as the village laundress, for she always had a plentiful supply of worn, used sheets for the shrouds. Her own mother had done this service, employing a young Sarah Sabey to help her; that young woman, now old, continued to help Charity, who had inherited the vital task.

Pulling at Charity's arm, to ensure that she was fully attended to, Goodwife Sabey was concerned about the lack of tapers – each body needed one for the folded hands, and the vicar had informed her rather testily that he had forgotten to order any from the chandler.

Responding to this dereliction of duty on Reverend White's part, Charity Munnings told her friend not to worry, for she would have words with the vicar. It just so happened, that both the village coffin and cart were in need of repair at the moment, and she would simply drop a hint that the repairs might take a long time – almost certainly as long as it would take for the tapers to appear.

William Gilbert, village carpenter, was very protective of his widowed sister and her son, so this hint about a lack of repairs being done was not a mere woman's idle threat; the vicar would not be able to ignore her and village politics being what they were, everyone would be aware that it was the vicar's lack of foresight that meant burials were being delayed.

Once at home, Benet was impatient for dinner to be served and over, so he could go the Butts with Thomas. Archery practice was a mixed blessing for the villagers; Benet's short sightedness often caused his arrows to fall anywhere but on the target.

'Liza smiled at his enthusiasm and asked what he would do if called upon to serve in the local militia and was not surprised that he was all for it – so long as he could stay with Thomas to look out for him. Benet looked up at her slyly, "He t t t t talks about you a l l l l lot you know; I think he wants you to b b b be his sweetheart." Benet gave a smirk.

"He can think what he likes," 'Liza told him, sharply, casting a frown at Mistress Munnings and her mother, as a warning to them to say nothing, "Who knows what will happen in the future, or even if we'll stay here."

Benet’s face dropped in surprise, “N n n n no ‘L L L Liza, don’t say that; you can’t go away and live elsewhere,” and he looked at his mother in panic.

“I didn’t say we were going away, and we might not, but then, who knows, we might return to London,” ‘Liza could not resist saying.

“With that b b black man who comes to see you?” Benet asked suspiciously.

“Edward? No, not Edward, although of course, he is very fond of both of us,” she glanced at her mother who was shaking her head at the teasing, which had gone on long enough. “Oh Benet, I’m only teasing you,” ‘Liza told him.

“W w w well I wish you wouldn’t” replied Benet fiercely, “I don’t think it’s f f f funny,” and he scowled.

“Please be quiet now both of you,” and Charity began to say Grace.

Chapter 10

An increase in the number of pedlars, keen to see if there was more money to be had with a Queen living in the village, was keeping all of the Inns fairly busy, but there was an increase in the number of fights, both with strangers passing through, as well as between the usual locals, which surprised no one. The stocks were occupied almost permanently, and three vagrants found without their 'V' brand were marched immediately to the forge to be given it. Robert Shelley was to be seen walking around the village in the barrel for being so drunk he missed all the Sunday services, and two men were sent to the justice at Huntingdon for blasphemy.

Not only was it a very busy time for the village constable, but he had also been given the task of walking all the roadways, to announce that the Queen would be present at the dole window between Tierce and Sext on the Feast of St James (that very day) and be pleased to help the villagers in any way she could. She had also sent a message via the constable that the daily gifts of food and flowers that she had been receiving had been appreciated by her and her household and she thanked them all, saying that she was grateful for their love and loyalty.

The laundry seemed to take longer than usual that morning, and 'Liza was glad of the opportunity to leave it and get a drink of water, but noticed her mother was not in her usual seat under the outhut, where the light was so good for sewing; she wandered indoors wondering if she was ill. Her mother was sitting on their bed, just under the window embrasure and was sewing something which 'Liza could see was a green silk pouch of some kind. On the bed cover lay a pair of eyeglasses.

"No!" 'Liza shrieked, "No, you cannot give the Queen the glasses my Abuelita wore!"

Her mother turned and frowned, "Will you stop that shouting Aliza. Your manners are appalling, I have failed to bring you up well; you act like one of the village hoydens!" She carried on stitching and, moving closer, 'Liza could see a pomegranate and underneath words in gold thread. Around the edge were small white crosses on a red background.

"Hun, hum?"

"Humilde y leal" her mother told her, "Humble and loyal, it is the Queen's personal motto. And no, these are not your Abuelita's glasses. Edward brought them to me last week and suggested that I give them to Her Majesty."

'Liza blinked, "How did he know she needs them?"

Hannah shook her head, "I have absolutely no idea."

"Are you going to see the Queen today? Can I come?"

Hannah put down the sewing and pointed to her snips, which lay on the chest at the foot of the bed, "Yes and yes but only if you behave yourself and, don't talk!" She snipped the thread and looked at her handiwork.

The perfectly formed letters stood out from the green silk beautifully, the tiny border of red and white emphasised them by drawing the eye to the words. Hannah smiled in satisfaction, before slipping the eyeglasses into the pouch, and placing it on top of the coffer.

'Liza slipped off the bed and went to the window to see what Benet was doing. He was standing by the wringing frames, waiting for her to rejoin him. Her shoulders slumped – today was one of those days when the birds were singing to her to go and walk in the fields or woods and do nothing. She sighed heavily.

Hannah came and stood beside her, slipping her arm around her daughter's waist, she gave her a hug, "I know you don't want to work today, but finish what you are doing as quickly as you can and then, I think we will go and see if we can give our gift to the Queen." 'Liza brightened up at once.

With that, mother and daughter went outside to resume their usual tasks. Charity Munnings, who had been folding the dried shifts and sprinkling them with lavender, had paused by the well and told Benet that, before he did anything else, that afternoon, he needed to sew up the largest cockerel's anus as she had planned to have a chicken stew when Goodwife Sabey came for dinner on Friday and if he didn't get on with it, the meat would not be fit to eat.

'Liza could never understand why this procedure made the chicken meat taste better, but that's what the villagers believed, so that is what they did, each time! Benet scowled, he hated the job, and it was always with difficulty that he persuaded 'Liza to do the sewing for him while he held the poor bird firmly – as not unnaturally it did not take kindly to any part of the operation.

'Liza hated doing it too, but she looked at it as one less cockerel to spoil her early morning sleep with its noisy crowing. She collected the bone needle and coarse thread from the small shed and waited for Benet to catch the bird. It seemed to know that something nasty was in store for it because it led Benet a dance around the garden, squawking its insults at him, until finally, he caught it up. 'Liza got to work at its back end and then stood safely to one side. Having pecked a large piece out of Benet's hand, which bled profusely, it waddled off, its little black eyes darting baleful looks back at them both.

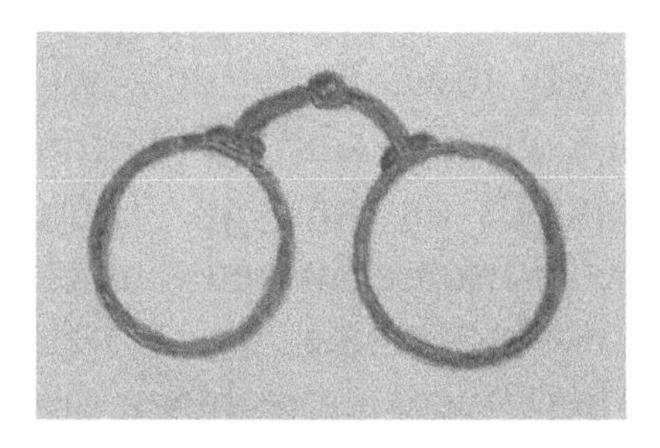

Chapter 11

The soldier searched the small cart diligently while Tom Carter stood patiently waiting, sucking his teeth. Boxes were rifled, bags felt and poked, baskets half tipped out. One package was covered in a fine red woollen cloth. “Here you!” Tom was suddenly stirred into action, “be careful with that packet!” as the guard poked the sharp tip of his halberd into the cloth, making a small hole, “that there comes from the Bishop himself, and it’s for his steward, not the Queen.”

The guard removed the point, hawked and spat onto the ground to show his disdain, while the other soldier picked it up and shook it, felt it all around and then dropped it back into the cart; the basket next to it contained a small tub of oranges, and one or two went missing as they were parted and sorted. Then with a nod at Tom he stepped back, and Tom was waved through the outer gatehouse.

The long line of villagers shuffled forward.

Once through the search at the gate, the queue meandered slowly towards the dole window in the inner gatehouse, giving 'Liza ample time to look at the black diamonds on the wall. There were very many of them, and some formed a black cross, as if you didn't know that the place belonged to a churchman. There were more black crosses on the Tower walls which loomed above the inner courtyard. The coat of arms outlined in the brickwork meant nothing to her.

In spite of their orders to supervise the villagers carefully, many of the guards were now lying on the grass near the moat, idly watching the straggling queue, and fighting to stay awake in the hot sunshine. They had given up trying to examine each and every basket and pouch, carried by the villagers who had come to pay their respects to the Queen of England, who remained an object of great curiosity and gossip to all of them.

'Liza was incredibly bored and looked longingly at the moat, for it was getting hotter by the minute. The light dancing off the water in the moat would dazzle your eyes if you looked at it for too long, but there was also something mesmerising about its movement, and it looked cool and inviting. The outer courtyard was a hive of activity, with grooms and servants going in and out of the many barns and stables, shouting to each other and taking no notice of the queue who were forced to dodge aside from men and beasts.

It was a relief to actually reach the shadow cast by the inner gatehouse and before she quite realised it, she and her mother found themselves at the head of the queue and facing Katharine, Queen of England.

The dole window set into the wall on the right-hand side, was shrouded in darkness and both of them blinked several times at the sudden loss of clear sight, which meant they barely made out the face of the woman in front of them, but she was smiling as she leaned slightly forward.

"Good afternoon, Mistress, and how may I help you?" her accented voice was slightly husky.

Hannah made a small curtsey, pulling 'Liza down next to her, then in Spanish she said clearly, "Su Majestad, he trando also que espera le ayudare a ver con mayor claridad."

'Liza looked in surprise from her mother to the Queen who looked positively shocked, while the man standing next to her, said "Good gracious me!" as he took a closer look at Hannah.

Hannah proffered the silk pouch through the window, only to have one of the soldiers at the side of the window step forward, "English only, Mistress if you please, and let me see that whatever it is," and he took the glasses' pouch.

"Your Majesty, I have brought you something which I hope will let you see more clearly," Hannah repeated in English.

Finding nothing suspicious, the soldier handed it through the window to the Queen who looked at it carefully, smoothing the lettering with her finger before removing the pair of eyeglasses. She looked at them for a few seconds then placed them on her face, turning her view one way and then the other before gently replacing the glasses in the pouch, which she handed to someone standing just behind her.

Queen Katharine smiled broadly at Hannah saying, "You are most thoughtful, Mistress?"

"Bakker," responded Hannah, making another curtsey.

"I admit that using my reading stone when I sew is becoming very tiresome to me." She paused and continued, "I must, that is, I would like very much to know how you came by the eyeglasses and also, how you speak Spanish so well, but I fear this is neither the place nor the time," and she turned to someone who, moving forward, 'Liza could see, was a man dressed all in black.

The Queen spoke rapidly in Spanish to him before she leaned forward once more,"I will send my physician Dr de la Sa to see you now and we can arrange for you to see me in the garden. Yes?" and seeing Hannah nod and curtsey again, she smiled and then dismissed them both with a slight wave of her hand.

The soldier jerked his head at them both while pulling Hannah to one side. Mother and daughter waited for a minute or two and then saw the black-dressed man beckon to them from the inner courtyard. Their place in the queue had already been taken by

Robert Shelley, whining about having to feed his hungry children, and unsurprisingly he was asking for money.

It was tempting to tell the Queen that this sob story would be a pack of lies and that the Shelleys were not to be credited with even a grain of honesty, but to do so would be dangerous. The family had several members, and they could pop up in the most unexpected places when you were on your own. They made poor friends but worse enemies.

The Queen's physician beckoned to them to come further into the inner courtyard, where he introduced himself in poor English and then asked them if it would be convenient for them both to visit the Queen, that day, in the cloistered garth some short time after Sext, but before Nones, for it being St James' day, the Queen wished to celebrate Spain's very own saint with a special Mass at Vespers.

Hannah, rather surprised at how easy it had been to speak with the Queen, gave a small curtsey to acknowledge him and his message and nodded. However, before she could say anything, Master White the steward, approached them, and looking somewhat embarrassed, spoke to them, "Mistress Bakker, I overheard the good doctor just now, and while I am happy that you can come and talk to Her Royal Highness the Princess Dowager," he gave a hard look at the doctor, "there will have to be someone with you the whole time. Of course, I am sure that it is unnecessary but, you understand, I have my orders."

Hannah murmured, 'of course', and glanced at the doctor before replying that they would both present themselves a little after Sext. She asked if Master White would alert the guards so that they would not keep the Queen (hastily changed to Princess Dowager as the steward started to protest) waiting, and then turned around.

Stopping to exchange a few words with some of the villagers in the still slow-moving queue, 'Liza had to wait until they were through the outer gatehouse, before whispering, "What will you do? You can't pass a message if someone is watching and listening all the time."

Hannah shook her head, "Don't worry Aliza, this has gone very well so far. I realise that the Queen must have been expecting something like the glasses and knows we are to be trusted to help her. I have already thought of a simple way to transport any messages and you should know that it will involve you. I'll explain fully after I have talked with the Queen this afternoon," and she tucked her arm through her daughter's and enjoyed being able to leave her daughter speechless for once.

Chapter 12

As commanded, Hannah and her daughter presented themselves at the gatehouse a little after Sext and were reluctantly allowed through it by the guards. However, the men turned the small willow basket which Hannah was carrying, containing her sewing things, almost completely upside down as though it might conceal something they couldn't easily see, and then made them wait while a message was sent to Lady Darrell.

She hurried towards them, smiling as she glided across the courtyard. Ushering them like wayward hens towards the cloistered garth; and told them in a slightly breathless voice how much the Queen was looking forward to their visit, and how good it would be for Her Majesty to hear news of the world from beyond these brick walls. She reminded them to address her as Your Majesty and wait until she had spoken first to them, then hesitating, she casually mentioned that Lord Mountjoy had forbidden anyone in the household to address the Queen as such.

"We ladies of course do not follow this instruction, for we were sworn to her service some time ago and hold to our oaths; I hope, that you will accord Her Majesty the respect she deserves?"

Mother and daughter assured her that they would be mindful of all that she had said. She also told them, casually, that Master White or one of the

Queen's English officers would be about and they were to speak in English – unless an opportunity arose to speak in Spanish, and she raised her eyebrows meaningfully.

She looked them both over, but Liza, who was wearing a fresh apron and cap, and Hannah, neat as a pin as always, looked presentable enough to meet a queen. Hannah tightly clutched the basket containing her small linen sewing bag (which housed some of her samples), a variety of threads and her needle case, as well as her mother's book of designs, but showed few nerves, while 'Liza was too worried that the book might be given to the Queen and was rehearsing a little speech in her head to say that it was far too precious to give away. She had decided though that the Queen was welcome to look at the book just for today.

Shown into the garth which lay between the Great Chamber, the Chapel and the Great Hall, they found the Queen already sitting there, sewing in the welcome shade cast by the roof, while scattered around her were her other ladies and their maids who were sewing also; it was a peaceful scene. One of the maids was as black as Edward Swarthye and 'Liza could not help but stare at her, wondering if perhaps those two knew each other, both were Moors and must have seen each other in London.

It seemed not, however, for when her mother asked that very question first of all, after the formal curtseys and introductions, they were told, "There is no relation to the needle maker; Senorita Isabella is my maid, and also my goddaughter," the queen smiled, "her mother was originally the maid to one of my most devoted ladies, Donna Salinas, who married the English Lord Willoughby, sadly, she is no longer with me." The Queen gave a small sigh, then crossed herself and muttered something under her breath. She gave a small smile saying, "Forgive me, it is hard not to think of myself, and I must not resent for my ladies their share of happiness."

Hannah told the Queen that there had been other Moorish families living in Cheapside, but that Edward Swarthye seemed the most successful. Queen Katharine nodded, "I know of this Edward the needle maker, but I can assure you that it is only their Moorish ancestry that he shares with my Isabella," she looked at the girl who was sitting across from them near an open embrasure, "Senorita Isabella will always find her home with me, for her own mother died some years ago," and the Queen crossed herself again.

"How sad," Hannah replied, also crossing herself.

'Liza and Isabella exchanged quick glances with each other before looking away.

"Ah, here comes Master White to ensure that you have nothing forbidden in your sewing bag, or your conversation," she added wryly, and the steward was indeed hastening out of the Great Hall toward them. "Master Steward," the Queen called, "I take it you will have no objection to these two young girls walking in the little park here? It would be good for Senorita Isabella to practise her English and to talk with someone of her own age."

"And for Aliza to practise her Spanish," Hannah responded swiftly, as she handed her bag to the steward who, like the guards, took everything out, riffled through the design book and then nodded at them both, leaving Hannah to retrieve everything and pick up the book ready to show to the Queen.

If he thought it odd that a village girl should keep company with one of the Queen's maids, the steward kept his thoughts to himself, merely telling them to stay inside the park, then bowed and left them, saying he would be back from time to time.

Isabella led 'Liza out of the garth back into the inner courtyard which gave entrance to the small park; her lovely red bodice and skirt almost glowed in the sunshine. The green heels of her fine leather shoes only seemed to scream 'you are a nothing' as 'Liza followed in her sturdy wood and leather clogs, while her brown skirts were not full enough to swish and sway and looked drab and serviceable even in the bright sun.

'Liza felt small and unimportant.

Chapter 13

Bella was walking quite quickly and with her head well down; behind her, 'Liza walked with increasing impatience until they were safely out into the park before saying, a little peevishly, to her back, "It wasn't my idea you know! And you don't have to speak to me in Spanish or English," she tossed her head, "I know, I'm only a simple village girl and far too unworthy to speak to a fine court lady like you." She muttered "snob" a little more loudly than she had meant to.

Isabella immediately stopped and turned round to face 'Liza, saying fiercely, "I am no persona pretenciosa, and I was not being rude. I just don't know what to say to you," she finished lamely. She gave a sigh and sniffed, "Of course, if the Queen wishes us to talk together then I will do so."

Bella looked at 'Liza and frowned. She continued, "The ladies and I, we were so surprised to hear your mother speak Spanish. Out here so far away from London, well, we, I, don't know what to think."

'Liza had never really meant for the girl to hear her insult and now felt rather ashamed of herself for she sounded truly apologetic. She looked at the Queen's maid and tried to think what she could say to smooth things over, so said hurriedly, "Maybe I was a bit hasty. Look I'll tell you a bit about myself and then you do the same. Then we won't have to worry about what we can say to each other, seeing as how we are so different anyway. Agreed?"

Isabella nodded slowly and they walked on together, but rather aimlessly into the park, where the trees spread some welcome shade. The royal maid was completely at a loss to know how to treat this village girl, for she rarely spoke to anyone not associated with the Queen's inner court. Her fine red skirts swished through the dry grass, with bits of leaf and soil adhering to the hem, and 'Liza couldn't help but envy such fine red cloth and the expensive, embroidered girdle which the girl was wearing. She had never had anything half as fine to wear.

'Liza sighed, and began, "My name is 'Liza, well really Aliza, Aliza Bakker. My name means 'joy', because Mami said my father Johannes was so happy when I was born after my brothers died. We used to live in London, but we had to move here a few years ago – after the sweating sickness killed my father and grandmother."

Isabella stopped walking and looked at her with much more interest, tipping her head slightly towards her, which seemed to be encouraging her, so 'Liza continued with the story of her grandparents leaving Cordoba and going first to Antwerp, where her own mother and father had met, and finishing with her mother and grandmother working as embroiderers. In London.

To all of this the Spanish girl listened attentively, occasionally brushing a fly away from her face as she concentrated on the story. 'Liza stopped and looked at her, wondering if she had said too much, or whether perhaps Isabella had not understood everything she had told her.

"Your turn now," 'Liza spoke a little hesitantly, unsure whether the girl would tell her anything about herself, or even talk to her.

Isabella sighed and there was a slight pause, as though she was deciding what to do, then, "My name is Isabella, and it means 'pledged to God.' Yes? But only the Queen calls me that; it's Bella to everyone else, and I know about the sweating sickness, because it killed my mother."

'Liza was stunned, for she had never expected that!

Isabella looked away from 'Liza into the distance, "It happened so quickly that one day she was with me and the next, she was gone, for ever." Her face creased slightly, and she blinked several times as memories of that time flooded into her mind.

What could anyone say in response to that? 'Liza thought.

Somewhere nearby, a bird trilled, and they both listened to it before Isabella continued, "She had come to England as a maid to Donna Maria de Salinas, who was lady in waiting to Her Majesty. You would not know this, but the Queen loved Donna Maria very much. Of course, my mother, being a Moor, was worried that she might not be made welcome here, but it was not so; she was very happy here and later married my father, Felipe. He had also come to England with the Queen – as one of her grooms. My mother said it was strange that she got married and then shortly after, Donna Salinas married the English Lord Willoughby."

"Your father," 'Liza began uncertainly, then finished, "was he a Moor too?"

"Yes, he was an expert at handling the Queen's horses. Everyone, even the English grooms and stable hands thought well of him and his work."

Bella frowned and paused as though reluctant to say more.

"What happened to him? Did he die of the sickness as well?" prompted 'Liza.

Isabella shook her head, "No he was killed in the May riots; it was before I was even born, so I never knew him," Bella crossed herself and brought her rosary up to her lips, to kiss it.

'Liza frowned as she cast her mind back to the time she lived in London - which was rapidly fading in her memory. She vaguely remembered riots occurring from time to time, for there was often trouble between the apprentices and foreign traders and their families.

Bella did not wait for her response, and explained, "It was in May 1518, a very terrible riot by the apprentice boys, and my father was one of those killed."

'Liza could hear the sadness in her voice and unthinkingly reached out and touched her arm, "I am sorry, truly sorry – I was twelve when my father died, and he was a wonderful father, and at least, I will always have happy memories of him."

The two girls walked on side by side, without speaking but both felt more at ease with one another. A shared troubled past had given them something in common at last.

"You know you are very lucky to have been able to know your father, and to remember him," Isabella broke the silence. "My mother told me that it was just the most terrible luck that he had gone out into London to fetch some leather for a saddlery repair, and of course there was no mistaking him for a foreigner! He tried to run from them, but," she gave a small shrug.

"Did your mother know she was with child?"

Isabella shook her head, "No, and she was heartbroken after he died of course. She decided to return to Spain when she knew she was having me, but Donna Salinas was very kind to her, and promised her that she and her child, would always be looked after. She even asked the Queen to be my godmother, to make doubly sure we would be fine."

'Liza was astonished – to have a Queen as your godmother!

Isabella sighed. "It was very difficult when Donna Salinas left the Queen to live with her English husband, and my mother worried constantly about also moving into a strange household with a small child to take care of, but the Queen immediately made my mother one of her very own maids of honour."

Isabella nodded at 'Liza, smiling, "We stayed at the court until the sickness came, and when my mother lay dying, the Queen sent word that she was to have no fears for me, for the Queen would take me as maid in her place, I would be looked after – always she promised. Her Majesty has kept that promise."

Her voice tailed off and 'Liza felt very sad for her, despite her expensive clothes and fine ways; Isabella had not had an easy life, even if it was richer and finer than anything 'Liza had known, for she had never had the ongoing love and security that 'Liza had experienced with her Mami.

'Liza turned to the Spanish girl, "I'm so sorry – truly I am sorry that you were left alone; I can't imagine what my life would be like if I did not have my mother," she spoke earnestly.

Isabella tucked her hands into her skirts, "It could have been far worse for me; I know I have been lucky because the Queen has looked after me always, and not just by giving me a home and work. You know that she believes all her ladies should read and write: to be able to read books which will improve them and show them the right way to live, and of course they must be able to help their husbands when they marry. So, I have also received an education thanks to her."

Perhaps she was not boasting, but it felt a little like it and 'Liza immediately responded proudly, "I too can read and my Abuelita taught me my numbers, so I do all the bills for Mistress Munnings. I am not an ignorante!"

Seeing the heat flood into 'Liza's face, Isabella held up a hand in a placatory way and then placed it on her heart, and slightly bowed her head, "I did not mean, I did not, please forgive me, I did not mean to boast of my good fortune or, judge you. Mea culpa. I will confess my pride to Father Abell, and I will ask God to forgive me; I am not used to, to," She stopped as if searching for what to say next.

"Talking to una plebeya?" Slightly mollified by this apology, 'Liza shrugged, "Well I suppose I am a commoner; I think we are perhaps both at fault for judging each other only by how we dress and where we live. You know you hold your head so high and walk so proudly and …what have I said now?"

Isabella had begun to laugh, covering her mouth with her hand and giggling, "You would not think me so high and mighty if you could see me practising walking with many books balanced on my head, and as I wobble all the time, the books, they fall!"

They walked slowly, but closer together now, and 'Liza informed her, "People are always quick to judge you by your clothes or where you live. I do understand about how difficult it can be to live among people who treat you suspiciously, just because you are different."

She glanced at the Spanish girl's face and then added, "You know it was the Queen's mother who forced my Abuelos to leave Cordoba. You understand that they were marranos, but the churchmen there did not believe they were truly

Catholic," here Liza stopped for a moment as she began to feel unsure of continuing this confession, "also my mother told me that some of their neighbours were very jealous of their business success, and they were happy to say spiteful things about them."

She stopped abruptly, for the truth was of course that her grandmother had never been a truly committed Catholic, but she could never tell Isabella that. It had been enough to say what she had, trying to show that she understood suspicion and the need to be wary when you are a stranger.

There did not seem to be anything else to say following this confession and they walked on in silence, until Isabella abruptly stopped and looked straight at 'Liza, "I wonder what it is the Queen really wants from us."

"I have been wondering about that too," 'Liza replied and managed to stop herself from saying any more. It had been on the tip of her tongue to tell Isabella what her mother had said following the visit from Edward Swarthye.

Isabella skipped on a little and then dropped her voice, saying, "My days are, well, often quite boring, I must not do this or go there or speak to anyone on my own; I must always behave correctly so I do not reflect badly on the Queen. Also, you already know Her Majesty goes to hear the services many times in the day, like today with an extra Mass to be said for Saint James; sometimes, I find my thoughts wandering when they should be devoted to God alone. I know the Queen would be shocked if I told her this." She looked anxiously at 'Liza who nodded at her and gave a sympathetic smile.

Another confidence shared.

'Liza wondered how to restore Bella's spirits and as they made their way out of the park, she described Benet in church and his sneezing fits and made her new friend laugh.

Chapter 14

They were now near to the Tower, which stood outlined against the blue sky, the rooks in the nearby trees cawing loudly as they took off and circled around it. The Spanish girl stopped abruptly and spoke firmly, as if she had come to a decision. "I am Bella, and I think we will be friends now and that will please Her Majesty, and me, si?"

'Liza smiled, "I am pleased to meet you Bella, I'm 'Liza." She held out her hand, which Isabella looked at for a second before grasping it in both of her own and squeezing it gently. And as they continued towards the Palace, both girls felt much happier than when they had left it.

"The eyeglasses will be good for the Queen," Isabella said suddenly, "although she hates to admit it, she has difficulty now with the tiny stitches, in any pattern, and often asks one of us to do them for her."

"My Abuelita wore such glasses – my Abuelo ordered them from Saint Catherine's Monastery, where the monks make them. She took them with her when she had to leave Spain, because her reading stone was not good enough for very fine work, just like the Queen; although my Abuelita always told me she only needed them because the light in Antwerp was poor, not bright like in Cordoba."

There was little activity to be seen in the courtyard, the air was so still that it felt as if everyone was asleep. They slipped into the cloistered garth near the Great Hall, without meeting a soul. Hannah and the Queen were sewing companionably side by side, murmuring softly in Spanish to one another, while one of the ladies was reading aloud the life of Catherine of Sienna, a favourite of the Queen's apparently, and one they had heard many, many times before, as Isabella whispered to 'Liza, rolling her eyes. Lady Darrell was sewing by the far entrance, keeping an eye open for Master White or any other member of the household who might invade the Queen's privacy.

Queen Katharine looked up as the girls approached her, and Isabella swept down in a graceful curtsey. 'Liza bobbed a kind of curtsey. "I hope you two have had a pleasant walk together. We mothers have decided that it would be good for you to do so once a week, so that you," 'Liza was addressed directly, "can practise your Spanish, which I hear, has been woefully neglected, and I think it will also be good for Senorita Isabella to have time away from us, to take some exercise in the fresh air. Subject to my requirements, I will release Senorita Isabella and send a groom to tell you when you may come here." The Queen had raised her voice, signalling for the reading to cease.

Seeing her daughter's face, Hannah hastily broke in, "Her Majesty is being both kind and gracious Aliza, and I heartily approve." Which actually meant that 'Liza should refrain from making any comment.

The bells began to toll for Vespers and knowing of the Queen's plans for Mass – to which she had been cordially invited, and to which she had regretfully declined, Hannah knew it was time to leave. The Queen took off her new eyeglasses and put them away carefully. She smiled and held out her hand for Hannah to kiss, before rising slowly to her feet, followed by her ladies who stood waiting patiently for her signal to leave. Isabella had already moved forward to pick up the Queen's sewing things and the royal entourage then swept out, leaving 'Liza and her mother the sole occupants of the garden.

The two of them made their way home, pausing to let the guards take a cursory look at the basket, and having left the sewing things in the house, they informed Benet that they were walking out to gather late blooming elder flowers, for Mistress Munnings was an excellent wine maker – and drinker – of several country wines, and elderflower was a favourite of her sister-in-law, Mary Gilbert. Benet merely nodded and carried on whittling a piece of wood.

Such a rare moment of privacy between the two of them, meant they could talk openly without fear of being overheard, and having reminded 'Liza about Edward's agreement with her, Hannah elaborated on the way the messages would be exchanged, warning that if discovered it would mean imprisonment or even death for them both and Bella who was the Queen's choice of go-between.

In essence, the walks with Isabella would allow them to give or receive a message away from the eyes of the guards and household officers – even the Queen's ladies would be ignorant of this, all that is excepting Lady Darrell. Such a message would always be a small piece of parchment that could be easily concealed, and Hannah intended to make a small pocket in the waistband of 'Liza's best apron, while Isabella would wear a light gold chain on her girdle, with a pomander at the end, which once unscrewed, would reveal a small hiding place. It was unlikely that they would be minutely searched so they should be safe.

"And then? You send it to Edward in a collar I suppose?" 'Liza asked.

"Yes, it will be easy to hide it inside there and John the Carter knows to take any parcel I give him and deliver it straight to Edward. I have no wish to know to whom he gives it, for the less we know the better."

The elder flowers were beginning to wilt, and they were forced to turn for home, with 'Liza torn between excitement at such daring in the face of authority, and a little frisson of fear at her part in it all. She wondered if her new friend Bella felt the same.

Chapter 15

Bella had indeed felt the same mixture of fear and excitement as 'Liza, when her role as go-between was explained to her after Mass. She also felt extremely proud that she was trusted by Queen Katharine to undertake this hazardous task.

Lady Darrell was at pains to warn her, "Be under no illusion, this is very dangerous; we are watched all the time and everything we do is noted. You must trust no one, especially Lord Mountjoy and certainly none of the English servants. Passing secret messages could put you in prison or even under sentence of execution; and similarly, the village girl and her mother will face the same penalty, if caught."

Isabella had looked up in consternation, so that Lady Darrell had to quickly add that, only in the seal of the confessional could she mention anything that was troubling her.

However, Bella quickly realised that her weekly meeting with 'Liza, even if there was no message, would break the claustrophobic routine that stifled her spirit, and, having found out about the girl's past, Bella felt that they would be friends and allies. She could talk to her and know that what was said, would remain secret between them.

For 'Liza, there was no difficulty in absorbing the need for secrecy: she had lived long enough in London and in the small community of outsiders in

Old Jewry to know how dangerous gossip could be. It was a bonus that Mistress Munnings and the villagers would never think she was capable of doing anything so demanding – she was just a poor, ill-educated village girl after all.

The cachet of one of her lodgers spending time with a member of the Queen's household had not been lost on the laundress, and she dropped a hint that any news from the Royal quarter would be well received by her. Since Hannah and her daughter knew that any information would be spread among her village friends, the village would always know something of what was happening in the Palace. 'Liza hoped that Bella would be able to give her some titbits of news, and so keep the laundress happy.

The week rolled on with its usual routines – although the well-dressed man at the Lion left just after the first alms-giving – satisfied that enough checks were in place to keep the Queen from any independent action.

Little did he know!

The Sunday service ended, and again, the Queen and her household did not put in an appearance. The villagers accepted that she would always stay within the Palace. Her piety and regular attendance at all daily services in the Palace Chapel were well known and only added to her peerless reputation. This religious duty contrasted well with the stories of the new Queen Anne and her activities at court, which was an endless source of gossip and speculation from the pedlars and chapmen who travelled the North Road.

Thomas and Alice elected to walk back with their aunt, forcing 'Liza to indulge in some manoeuvres to keep away from Thomas. He was not ill-looking, and she knew him to be kind and courteous, but she had no intention of marrying him, and was determined to make him realise this and look for someone else. Rebecca at the dairy, for instance, had told her that she had been in love with Thomas since they were both small and 'Liza felt that she would make him an ideal wife.

Alice was chattering on and on about the number of corn dollies she had made for the fields, ready for Lammas. Strictly frowned on by the Church of course as being a throwback to pagan days, but a country tradition that the villagers adhered to, regardless. Every field would have one placed discreetly at one of its corners.

Goodwife Taylor had been tasked with the baking of the harvest loaf from the first of the new wheat that had been specially milled by Simon Fox up at the village mill, and she was already looking forward to leading the procession in the church, of villagers bearing gifts.

Meanwhile, Thomas was loudly explaining his money-making scheme at great length to Hannah, whereby he sold butter and cheese moulds to travellers at the White Horse and the Crown, thanks to his cousins who ran those inns. He carved them from lumps of sycamore wood left over from other carpentry jobs.

Even 'Liza acknowledged his talent at carving and knew that Benet tried to copy him when he whittled any piece of wood. However, Thomas was really more concerned to speak loudly enough for 'Liza to hear how well he was doing at making money, for he had vowed that he would make her see him as a potential husband.

'Liza was not looking forward to going to church again so soon - Lammas was a holiday for all, but there was Mass at church of course when the first fruits were taken in to be blessed. It made the service even longer than normal and always made 'Liza wonder how many fruit pies and tarts the vicar ate afterwards!

Charity Munnings was remarking to Hannah that Ann Serle was looking crumpsey and must be expecting again; it meant that John's extra work harvesting the grain, would be a welcome boost to the Serle income. John Serle had been working over in Sturtlow for much of the hay harvest which had now finished and would be looking for more work to follow on. Hannah murmured somcthing or other in reply, but she was not really listening.

The celebration of Lammas superseded the planned walk and Bella and 'Liza were both disappointed; it was fortunate that no message had arrived from Edward as yet, and equally there was nothing from the Queen.

The Transfiguration of Christ fell on the following Sunday and the villagers were encouraged to attend the all-night vigil beforehand. 'Liza did not go, although Alice and her mother attended.

At the Palace there was never any question that the Queen and her court would not be attending the vigil through the night. For most of the time, the Queen knelt on the stone floor, her hands clasped around her rosary and her eyes closed, while Father de Athequa read the lessons and prayers, and asked them all to contemplate the Light of the World. It was a very long night for Isabella, who was profoundly relieved when the light of the sun crept through the windows, and she and the others were allowed to get some rest before the long Mass to come later that morning. The Queen stayed where she was.

Chapter 16

The weather continued to be sunny but without the heavy heat of July, and for the next two Tuesdays, the girls met in the inner courtyard first under the watchful eye of Lord Dymock, the Queen's almoner, before being allowed to walk into the park; he accompanied them for a few minutes, but their conversation was about nothing important enough to keep his attention, and he dismissed their conversation as meaningless, and left.

Her mother had told 'Liza that this close observation of both girls would soon disappear and just to ignore anyone who was nearby when they met. The officers of the household had more important things to do than spend time over the tittle-tattle between two young girls, and so it proved.

By the third meeting, 'Liza was merely acknowledged by one of the men or one of the ladies in waiting. The initial shyness between the girls had completely vanished, aided in part by the few jumbles that 'Liza had managed to keep from the guards' thieving hands. They would find a shady spot amongst the trees where they could chat, eat or doze, depending on how they felt.

For Isabella it was very near to being the most wonderfully peaceful time she had ever experienced, while 'Liza just enjoyed being away from the house, the washing and the various daily jobs, and just being alone with her thoughts.

In the previous week, Bella had passed on one message and a small item of news – speaking softly to 'Liza (while she stowed the message safely in the apron waistband) that the Queen was very worried, because she feared King Henry was planning to take away all her marriage dower lands and properties, and that he would reduce her income yet again. Money was a constant problem, Bella said and 'Liza told her that it was the same problem in every house in the village, including her own!

It was on the third outing, and after flinging herself on the ground, that 'Liza undid her apron and eased out a small packet from her waistband. She handed it to Bella with a meaningful look; the other girl solemnly took it and placed it carefully in the pomander, screwing on the top tightly, before taking something from her skirt pocket. Neither girl attempted to speculate on what might be in the message.

Bella then placed the something on 'Liza's apron. It was a small white square and when 'Liza picked it up she automatically smelled it. Bella smiled, "This is Jabon de Castile, a soap from Castile. We ladies use this soap for our skin, and I think you will like it. It is very expensive, but the Queen loves it and is still allowed to receive it, as a regular gift from the Lady Willoughby who would like very much to return to the Queen's service, now she is a widow."

"What is it made from?" 'Liza asked, thinking how different it was to the lye soap or even the soapwort they used at home.

"It is made with olive oil. You do not grow olive trees here, I think. The oil is why it is so soft. You like it?"

It was wonderful and 'Liza nodded enthusiastically. She could not help fingering it all the time and said "thank you" more than once. Bella responded casually that perhaps next time 'Liza could bring some more yumbles – she meant jumbles.

The deal was struck to the satisfaction of both; although Bella had to confess that the soap could not be a weekly gift, but there was no reason why the jumbles could not be shared weekly! The soap was very expensive, and she had had to cut her own bar in half to give some to 'Liza, who was touched. It was truly a generous gift from the Spanish girl, which singled her out as her friend, and she said so, which made the Spanish girl smile happily.

Bella, pleating her skirt between her fingers, told her,"I have never had a friend of my own age before, and I have never trusted anyone as much as I trust you. Of course, we hold each other's lives in our hands, and that of the Queen," her voice trailed off.

'Liza nodded, "I know; my mother and me both, and you. We are an unholy trinity!" and they both laughed before Bella covered her mouth with her hand, shaking her head and saying that that was blasphemy.

'Liza shook her head at that. The other girl's piety reminded her of Alice, and she told Bella about her friend and her decision to become a nun. Bella thought that the Queen would be delighted to know this and resolved to tell her as soon as she returned to the Palace.

The rest of their time was spent half dozing in the warm sunshine, their backs supported by one of the oak trees, so that they resembled nothing so much as a couple of small statues.

Later, as 'Liza sauntered through the outer gatehouse, her smile and obvious good humour caught the attention of the guard. "What's you been up to then?" he demanded, stepping in front of her.

'Liza showed him the small piece of soap and he took it from her, looking at it back and front, frowned, then scratched his head. "Wimmin!" he spat on the ground as he handed it back and smiling to herself, 'Liza skipped out of his way and home.

Throughout the rest of August, life followed the busy schedule of harvest – into the fields by sunup, cutting and stooking and threshing and sheaving. Most villagers, children included, were involved in one or other of the tasks of bringing in the grain. The evenings were beginning to darken earlier and there were times when rain stopped the work, either for part or all of the day, but fortunately it failed to stop the harvest being completed and this year, it was a good one.

There had been two more exchanges of messages, which were quickly accomplished leaving time to enjoy being out in the park as the two girls continued to enjoy the freedom to be themselves. Bella informed her that 'Liza's news about Alice had made the Queen very happy to hear of such vocation and that Her Majesty wanted to give Alice a small token of this pleasure. 'Liza and Alice were told to come to the dole window that following Tuesday to receive this gift.

"It's one of her rosaries," Bella confided, "she has many and this is one she was given when she lived in London. It has beautiful black polished stones with small pearls."

"Alice will love it."

The turning of the year prompted Bella to think about the onset of Autumn, and she voiced her concerns about what would happen in the winter months when the weather meant they could not walk without getting wet, muddy and cold. 'Liza told her not to worry for she had mentioned this to her mother and Hannah had already spoken to Lady Darrell; the Queen had agreed that when the weather was bad, Bella could visit 'Liza at the Munnings' house, as long as Hannah was present at all times, and she had to collect the girl herself and bring her back to Lady Darrell. Steward White had approved the arrangement.

This made Bella clap her hands together so vigorously that 'Liza thought it best to warn her that the house she would visit was poor, nothing like the rooms she was used to, and that she would have to prepare herself for the curiosity of both Benet and his mother.

Hannah hoped they would all be able to sit under the outhut rather than in the smoke-filled hall or kitchen, but Bella would need to bring a warm cloak with her, for sitting in the outhut, open as it was on three sides, would be a cold experience.

"The Queen gave me a warm woollen cloak with a beaver hood last year and I have a fur muff for my hands. I used to wear them all to the church services last year." She sighed, "I feel the chill in this country. The fires here at the Palace are not so well stocked and are lit quite late, I sometimes wonder if it is a deliberate plan to keep us uncomfortable. But I am lucky, poor Lady Darrell suffers many chilblains in the cold weather."

"Goodwife Sabey, who helps Mistress Munnings lay out the dead - she suffers from them too. She swears by bread and water poultice every night, but I've also seen her stuff her leather boots with wool as well," 'Liza told her.

Bella laughed, "I can't see Lady Darrell putting a bread and water poultice on her heels! She does have some ointment from Doctor de la Sa, and she has furred boots, but she still finds them painful."

A squirrel suddenly ran down the trunk of a tree beside them, stopping abruptly as it caught sight of them. Its red ears quivered with anger, and it chattered loudly as if telling them off for being there, before scurrying back up the tree, causing both girls to smile at such a show of indignation.

It reminded Bella of the small capuchin monkey that had been a pet of the Queen's, and she made 'Liza laugh with her tales of Charia, and how it had torn many tapestries by climbing up them while the guards poked at it, in a vain attempt to force it down; it would shriek at ambassadors and lords, and more than once, pee'd on the king's black velvet slippers when he had been listening to music.

Her only experience of life was bound up with the routine of the Queen's personal daily life, and she spoke about it often; there were other, more personal snippets too: how the Queen wore a rough wool habit next to her skin, hidden from view by her velvets and silks, for she had long ago joined the Third Order of Saint Francis.

'Liza shook her head at this, such sacrifice of personal comfort was quite beyond her.

Isabella sometimes helped Lady Darrell to wash the Queen's hair, flecked now with white streaks, which she covered with ornate hoods, and said she had been shocked by the sores that the wool shift created on the Queen's skin. It was nothing she had been informed, when compared to the suffering of the Lord Jesus Christ.

'Liza sympathised with Bella's endless attendance at services in the chapel; but was quite shocked to hear that the Queen fasted each Friday and Saturday, taking only a mouthful of water throughout the day, and before and during all feast days belonging to the Blessed Virgin Mary. It was hard on the rest of her ladies, although they tried to share some of this devotion to God. They were forced to eat small meals in secret so that the Queen would not know, or even worse, be faced with the smell of food. Isabella gave a heavy sigh.

"I suppose she will fast on Friday, then, as it is the Nativity of the Virgin? At least it isn't an extra day, not if she always fasts on Fridays anyway."

Bella sighed, "It means she will want to fast from midday on Thursday and there will be even more services on the actual day, for she is devoted to the Madonna. She will go to Matins and stay in the chapel until Prime and one of us must stay with her. I find it very difficult to do this for such long periods, although I ask for strength to follow her example."

'Liza patted her arm, "You are doing all you can for her – don't forget – in all sorts of ways. I think you are very brave. I mean, I couldn't stop eating like you have to do." She racked her brains for something to take Bella's mind from her duties and eventually responded by telling some stories about the village and who was rumoured to be doing what and when and with whom.

'Liza thought about the Queen a lot that Sunday as she stood next to her mother, it being the twelfth one after Trinity, the Prebend of Lincoln Cathedral was tasked with preaching; he had arrived on the Saturday and made himself known to the Queen – to the Princess Dowager as he insisted on calling her.

'Liza heard later from Bella that his audience with her had lasted for as long as it took him to address her as "Your Royal Highness," before the Queen informed him that she was "a daughter of Spain and the King's true wife" and as such she was Her Majesty, the Queen of England and left him standing quite alone in the Great Chamber.

Chapter 17

September brought a variety of fruits and berries, which with the mushroom picking, demanded daily forays into the fields and woods to gather as much as they could. But these were also the cooler days; the sun set earlier and earlier, and after the Equinox, the nights seemed to rush to take over from the daylight.

Quarter-day, which was also the feast of Saint Michael, would see the usual busy hiring and firing of labourers and other servants, and rents paid – or not. Master Linton from the big house at Sturtlow, was at the green and hiring extra help to replant some of the hedge ends on the fields near his house, and John Serle was glad of the opportunity to earn more money. Ann had been very unwell during this pregnancy and had been unable to work very much for Mistress Munnings.

As usual, 'Liza was given time away from the laundry to gather baskets of blackberries which were in abundance this year – Goodwife Sabey told her that this was a sign of a bad winter to come. She soon grew weary of the task though, for as well as receiving numerous scratches on her arms and hands, and rips on her clothes, she often ended up ensnared in the prickly branches. There was no sympathy from Mistress Munnings when she moaned, she just told her sharply, "You eat the jam, so don't complain!"

Knowing of the regular walks in the park, Mistress Fauconer had sent Kitchen Agnes with the two girls that week to gather in some of the quinces and medlars that were ripening in the orchard, and with a basket of which later, 'Liza was paid for her effort.

Kitchen Agnes was not too sure about keeping company with Senorita Isabella, a royal maid! However, once back at the Palace or in the village, she earned more than one cup of ale when she told her story about being with 'the black maid of the Queen's'. It was sad but true that several villagers still wondered about Isabella, and there were some weird stories still circulating as to whether the black came off her skin when she washed, or if anyone knew if she could actually speak, or just grunted. This made Agnes roll her eyes and soundly berate them for such foolish thoughts.

Hannah and 'Liza also did their best to dismiss such fancies when they heard them, but were not always believed – after all, they themselves were foreigners. Many still stuck to their wild ideas even when soundly told off by Charity Munnings for voicing such foolishness and disrespect – as though the Queen would have a servant who was not excellent in every way!

On this particular meeting day, 'Liza was talking about the news brought to the village by some of the pedlars, that the Nun of Kent had been arrested, along with some senior churchmen who had supported her denunciation of the King, for presuming to divorce his wife, Queen Katharine. There was a lot of ignorant speculation about what would happen next, fed in no small part by rumours brought up the road by the many traders and pedlars.

Bella remarked that the Queen at least could rest easy, for she had never had any association with the nun, Elizabeth Barton – a point the Queen had been anxious should be fed into the village gossip circle, just in case anyone was suspicious of her. Whatever her innocence in the matter, it remained an extra worry for the Queen who feared that Henry would try to involve her with this latest evidence of treason in some way.

With one basket completely full, Bella had played with her pomander, partially screwing and unscrewing it, effectively giving notice that there was a message inside; so 'Liza sent Agnes back to the kitchen laden down with one full basket of medlars, telling her that Mistress Fauconer had given instructions for Agnes not to be away long (the night soil collectors were delivering a cartload of dried manure for the kitchen gardens, and it was Kitchen

Agnes' job to supervise them). Agnes was told that she need not rush back, but to reassure the housekeeper that they would fill the remaining three baskets, one of which 'Liza would take home as payment.

The baskets full, and the small piece of parchment safely handed over to 'Liza, and secreted in the apron band, the two girls lingered for a time among the trees of the orchard. Bella described the depression shown by the Queen, who was heartbroken at still being prevented from seeing her daughter, and despairing of Mary's demotion as a Princess, now that the King had named his new daughter Elizabeth as Princess Royal.

Such an honour given to a child of Anne Boleyn was not only a grave insult to Queen Katharine, but Princess Mary had been told that she would be sent to Hatfield Palace to act as a servant to this baby! Bella told her that this had made the Queen incandescent with anger and frustrated beyond bearing, that she could do nothing to restore her daughter's position at court.

"Eventually, she decided to send the Princess Mary one of her books – 'De Vita Christi', with a letter telling her to dedicate herself to God and to accept life's struggle with good grace; she hoped it would bring the Princess some comfort and was informed by Lord Mountjoy that he was only going to send it because the letter had been telling the Princess to be obedient. Can you imagine, he then suggested that obedience was a virtue that it behoved even Queens to observe!"

Listening to this emotional outpouring made 'Liza glad to be a simple villager. Tales of the incredible power struggle at the London court were brought into the inns by travellers and merchants, as well as the many lives that were affected by it, but this was too much for anyone to make sense of. 'Liza murmured that perhaps the message from the Queen was for her daughter, to tell her not to lose hope. Bella shook her head and shrugged; she never knew what the Queen wrote.

The weather broke the day after they had gathered these baskets of fruit from the Palace orchard, and it rained and rained and rained. The water cascaded off the roof turning the garden into a quagmire and the pig pen into a swamp; the chickens pecked forlornly at the muddy ground, their feathers wet and bedraggled, and the house seemed to chill instantly.

Mistress Munnings was forced to dry the laundry inside the small barn, which meant it took much longer to finish every order. It was fortunate that Thomas that summer, had built and fitted several 'winter hedges,' the wooden hangers over which the wet linen was draped, nevertheless it took a long time for the laundry to completely dry out.

John Serle passed by the barn on his way home early from work. He told them the remaining barley was fair knickled with all this rain and it was no good cutting it. He was off up the Brickle to help the cooper finish an order for barrels, and mentioned that Ann was still unable to do much, and the children were very hungry, which prompted Mistress Munnings to give him a pot of peas and beans cooked in bacon for them – and brushed off his thanks with a wave of her hand.

The dried sheets which were waiting to be returned, had to be protected from the rain by leather covers which had been heavily greased with tallow, and it was fortunate that Benet had finished doing this very job the day before the rains came. Another leather cover was around 'Liza's shoulders as she trundled the wheeled box full of linen to the Lion.

Opposite her at the smithy, Simon Fox, the miller, was sheltering under the roof waiting for his horse to be re-shod. He shouted a greeting at her, in fact he shouted all the time, which Mistress Munnings said was because of the noise of the millstones grinding away, but he was a cheerful man who was always ready to help others. 'Liza felt sorry for the horse though, for the poor animal spent its days walking round and round with the mule, forcing the stones to grind on each other and anything between them, on any day when the wind did not blow hard enough for the sails to turn.

She was glad to complete her job and dash home, but despite the leather cover, she was soaked to the skin and her skirt and legs were splashed with mud. Her shoes were sodden, and altogether she felt totally miserable as she huddled in front of the fire in the kitchen, with her hands around a horn cup full of warmed, spiced ale which Hannah had given to her as soon as she returned. She gave a huge sneeze at the same moment as her stomach growled and she hoped there was something good to eat for supper.

They sat around the kitchen table for their meal, but only Benet was talking – he was most concerned that the weather would not allow the harvest festival, due that first Sunday of October, for it would mean there would be no feasting and merry making after Church. He asked 'Liza if she thought the Queen would come.

Liza shook her head, her mouth full of bread and cheese, and it was her mother who answered him, "I don't think so Benet – it is not the kind of feasting and dancing she is used to! I did ask if Senorita Isabella might come with us, but Her Majesty has refused permission. I understand why, but it is a pity, as I think Bella would have enjoyed the music and seeing something of the villagers enjoying themselves, and we would make sure we returned here, before it all turned into the usual drunken mess."

Chapter 18

The double celebrations of the church's own dedication day, and the safe gathering in of the harvest had got dreadfully out of hand. At the start of the day, when the villagers had dutifully attended church and been passive onlookers as the harvest foods were offered, all had been quiet and seemly, until the vicar had preached an unusually long sermon (even for him) and the villagers grew more and more restive as he droned on.

A few of the smaller children wet themselves. Shuffling and coughing became more and more noisy, and the churchwardens were forced to patrol the nave, seeking out the worst offenders. Released at last, the men and women erupted boisterously from the church porch.

A lucky few had been busy since sunrise, placing benches and tables on the green, setting up the firepits and erecting the spits. Pork and beef sides were already roasting and filled the air with delicious smells. Benet had sworn he could smell the aroma of food inside the church, but that was probably an exaggeration. The major landowners had donated meat and bread and some ale, and everyone was impatient to take advantage of their generosity.

All the village brewhouses had been working every hour for the past week in anticipation of the demand for their ale, and the inns had stockpiled as many barrels as they could gather so that they would not miss out any extra income.

On the green, a fiddler and a couple of shawm players were keeping up a constant stream of dance music, aided by large tankards of ale, which were refilled as quickly as they were emptied. Food and drink disappeared rapidly, and the villagers swiftly got to the stage of dancing any steps whether or not they belonged to that dance, while others were whirling about with no sense of direction, just glad to be able to enjoy a day of pure pleasure with no work.

Children ran about in and out of the crowd, some of them crying with tiredness as they looked for their parents, others whooping and shouting to each other, barging their way backwards and forwards. Quite a few bodies lay on the ground, eyes closed, snoring with mouths open. A lethal combination of happiness and ale had caused the noise level to rise, and shrieks of laughter were augmented with shouting and roaring; unfortunately, some of it was not friendly, and the constable had been forced to put two people in the stocks by mid-afternoon.

It was just as well that Isabella had not come, Hannah thought, as she looked at the scene around her, knowing that the girl would have been horrified and fascinated in equal measure. 'Liza remained at her mother's side throughout the day and they both relied on Benet to get them some food. Hannah had prudently brought some water with her.

On the roadway, the first pig's bladder had split open, and several boys were sent off in search of another football. Some couples went missing and others quarrelled among themselves and with anyone else who happened to be nearby.

It was the usual harvest day celebrations.

Hannah's foot tapped in time with the music, but she was on the alert for any foolishness and had even forbidden 'Liza to dance with Thomas, much to his disappointment, and 'Liza's relief. He had asked quite properly, he thought, although his flushed face and bright eyes had betrayed just how much he had been drinking. 'Liza had been very pleased to be spared any possible embarrassment.

By late afternoon, Charity Munnings was searching for Benet, who had slipped away from her as soon as he could, and, as he was very poor at holding his drink, would have wandered off and fallen asleep somewhere, so she feared she would be searching for him with a torch. John Bateman, the Bishop's deer-keeper was already having to be carried home.

Charity went to enlist the help of her brother and sister-in-law in the search for Benet, and on joining her, they gave their daughter, Alice, into Hannah's care; she too had no taste for the rough antics the others called dancing, although she was enjoying her last look at raucous village life before she left them all, but a look was all she wanted.

'Liza shouted to her that the Queen wished to see her at the next almsgiving day at the dole window, and Alice was immediately curious as to why, but 'Liza had promised not to spoil the surprise and merely shrugged in reply.

As the noise level rose even further and several drunks wandered in and out of view, Hannah decided now would be a good time to make their way home; in addition, the evening was getting quite cool, and she was beginning to feel chilled. She had no wish to stay to eat meat that had been razzled, and the drunkenness was beginning to get out of hand.

On their way back down the road they watched Master Baccon (the village butcher) who had lost one of his shoes, walking in a dot and go gait as he attempted to stay upright. "I think it was the right time for us to leave, Aliza. Alice will stay with us until Mistress Gilbert comes for her," Hannah said firmly, and pushed them to move faster and leave the shrieks and cries and wail of the music behind them. Charity was nowhere to be seen so they slipped away into the dusk.

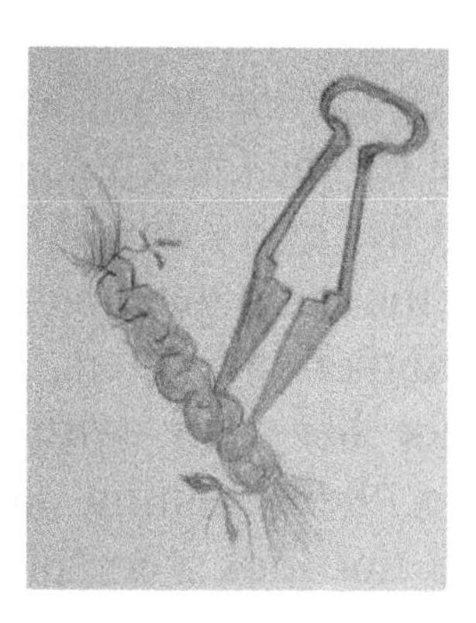

Chapter 19

As had been requested the previous month, 'Liza presented Alice to the Queen, at the dole window, by introducing her as one who would soon profess her calling to be a nun; 'Liza bobbed a curtsey while her friend, overcome with nerves, just stared at the Queen of England like a frightened rabbit and forgot to curtsey until pulled forcibly down.

Proffering the rosary, which had been wrapped in a small square of lawn, the Queen leaned forward and said, "You are entering into service of the Lord, and you have my prayers and good wishes; I counsel you to always choose sorrow for when you are happy you forget about spiritual things, you forget about God. But in sorrow He is always with you," then she paused, before finishing by saying quietly, "I know this to be true in my own life. I want no thanks, but I ask you to always remember me in your daily prayers."

Alice thought she would faint, she was so overcome. 'Liza curtseyed again and said that her friend was grateful for the Queen's gift and of course she would pray for her every day. Alice rushed home as soon as she left the outer gatehouse, eager to show the rosary to her mother and sisters.

'Liza arrived for her walk with Bella and was dismayed to see her waiting alongside Lord Mountjoy. He did not look very pleased and for a moment 'Liza felt a panic rise up inside her and became very conscious of the parchment nestling inside her apron. 'What if' she began to think.

The Chamberlain stamped his feet a little and told 'Liza to hurry up, he had been most remiss, he told her, allowing the girls to walk together for so many weeks with no supervision. His long, blue woollen cloak was wrapped across his shoulders, and he had pulled a large velvet cap down over his head. Next to him, Bella had hidden inside her fur trimmed hood. 'Liza felt a rush of relief that this was just a check on their conversation and hurried up, stumbling slightly in the new wooden clogs which covered her shoes.

Conscious of the eavesdropper behind them, Bella began to intone the life of Catherine of Siena – in Spanish – which she knew by heart. Pausing every so often to ask 'Liza if she had understood or needed help with the understanding. 'Liza just about managed to appear as if she had been learning Spanish all along.

The park was now strewn with the signs of Autumn – leaves lay in heaps along their way, blown into untidy heaps by the fickle breeze and the many trees and bushes would soon be bare. The berries on the hawthorn and the hips on the rose briar had taken their usual brilliant colour and 'Liza thought Goodwife Sabey might be right about this winter being a harsh one.

They rounded the first corner of their usual route when Lord Mountjoy ordered them to stop. "I am satisfied with your conduct," he told them pompously, "but I have important matters awaiting me, so you may continue your walk without me." He turned abruptly.

Bella continued with the Spanish until she knew he was completely out of sight, then stopped. They both breathed a sigh of relief and, having expressed her fear that he was going to find out about the messages,'Liza handed over the latest missive to her friend.

She told Bella about Alice and the rosary giving and how Alice had been struck dumb.

Bella put the message safely away saying, "I have seen this often – when the people first meet Her Majesty, and she is kind and generous to them. They expect her to be proud and cold and they are so surprised by her warmth and generosity that they end up stuttering or saying nothing; I could tell you many stories of how loved she is by the people of this country. Oh! I am so happy that horrid man has left us, you know both Lord Dymock and Lord Mountjoy refer to her as the Princess Dowager and, of course, she will not speak with them."

'Liza handed her some jumbles and Bella nibbled at one, then added, "Lord Mountjoy is no longer happy to be the Queen's Chamberlain here – he has been ordered by the King to ensure that we no longer address Her Majesty as the Queen but as Her Royal Highness, the Princess Dowager. He told us the King is making himself head of the church in England and so has no need take any notice of the Pope. I think he is distressed by the fact that the King will be excommunicated, while the Queen fears for the King's very soul,"

'Liza could only shake her head at all this.

Bella crunched her last jumble and sighed, drawing her hood closer round her neck. Under her black velvet cap, the golden net covering her jet-black hair sparkled in the sun, but 'Liza could see there were one or two holes in it where perhaps a finger had torn it, and she offered to take it back to her mother to be repaired. Bella hesitated for a moment then tugged it off her hair and handed it to 'Liza.

"I'm not surprised it's torn if you rip it off your head like that!"

Bella made no reply as she stuffed her hair under her cap, hoping it would stay up long enough for her to get to her room and find another net, for the Queen was very particular about the appearance of her ladies and maids, and with pins in her mouth she was unable to talk for a minute or two, but as they returned, she told 'Liza some of the rumours that were coming into the Palace, and none of them good for the Queen.

The wind had become stronger and colder, and she could see that 'Liza was suffering from the cold, while she only remained concerned that the pins in her cap would not hold her hair, and so as they parted, she warned 'Liza to wear something warmer next time.

'Liza went home to give the message and the net to Hannah, then proceeded to the Gilberts' house, where Alice was getting ready to leave for her new life as a nun on the following day. The family were still marvelling over the gift of the rosary when Liza arrived at the back door.

The Gilberts lived in a much bigger and grander house than most villagers, as befitted a prosperous tradesman and master carpenter. William had more than one workshop, two journeymen and two apprentices, one of whom was his son, Thomas. There were three small, thatched barns in which he stored his timber, and his land supported pigs and chickens and two vegetable plots which were where he went to relax, and be on his own, although he let his wife think it was for him to plan any commissions he had received. His wife was just happy for him to keep the family larder stocked with a variety of vegetables.

The family dogs greeted 'Liza's knock with loud barking from their kennel by the door, while one of the family cats shot through the opening as soon as the door was pulled ajar.

In the kitchen, lit by several smoky tallow candles, and near the window embrasure, Alice sat very still on the hard wooden bench, partly to quell the nervousness at what she was about to go through. She had pressed her knees tightly together and was gently twisting a few strands of her beautiful blonde hair between her fingers; the rest of it cascaded like a silky curtain down her back. She whispered a 'hello' to her friend and Thomas made room for 'Liza on the settle next to him. 'Liza sat as far away from him as possible, but gradually Thomas edged nearer and nearer. Were it not for the presence of so many members of the family around them, she would have stormed off.

Alice was frantically blinking back tears and sniffing loudly, as her mother made a loose plait and then took up the small shears and slowly snipped the plait away from the base of her daughter's neck. It dropped with barely a thud onto the floor where little Grace the youngest daughter, carefully picked it up, tying some twine around both ends to keep it secure. She held it up to her mother, who was watching Alice as the girl shook her head from side to side, feeling its unaccustomed weightlessness. Mistress Gilbert was filled with a mixture of pride and sadness at the girl sitting in front of her, and although she had sworn not to be overcome, she found her eyes full of tears and only just managed to control her need to cry.

Just behind her, 'Liza watched the proceedings in total silence. She had always been so jealous of Alice's beautiful hair, so unlike her own wild, dark brown, wavy hair which struggled to stay inside her coif. To cut such an asset! 'Liza would never had done it, but then, she reflected, she would never have wanted to be a nun either.

Alice turned around, looking a little shocked and slightly tearful, causing her brother Thomas to immediately give her a broad smile, and say, cheerfully, "You'll be the prettiest nun at Hinchingbrooke, and everyone is going to be jealous of you with that wonderful rosary you will wear. Just think," he stopped abruptly, as his mother shushed him.

She bent down to take the limp plait from Grace's hand and snapped, at him "If you have nothing better to do, Thomas, you'd best be getting back to work. Prioress Wylton will be honoured to have our Alice for her faith not her looks, nor her rosary!" She wiped her eyes with her apron and sniffed loudly.

Alice was really crying now, silently. Fat teardrops were rolling down her cheeks as the enormity of what she was about to do, hit her. Little Grace suddenly gave a loud wail and as her mother wrapped the blonde plait in a piece of linen, she started to cry too. 'Liza was already choked up and she had to keep shaking her head to stop herself from sobbing, which also was making her throat ache.

"I can't believe I'm losing my friend tomorrow and I'll never see you again" she whispered quietly to herself but was overheard.

Hearing her, Grace began to wail even more loudly, which prompted Thomas to get up from the bench and escape back into the male world of his father's workshop. He was busy carving a cradle from rowan wood – a particular request from John Burges, one of the larger landowners in the village. His father shouted occasionally and some of the workmen could be loud and rude, but at least there was a calmness there, which was a world away from the emotional scene taking place in the kitchen.

His father was finishing a large oak bedding chest – his family's gift to the Prioress for allowing Alice to become a Benedictine nun; it had a carving with the likeness of little Grace on one of the angel heads that decorated it and Thomas hoped the sight of it would always remind Alice of her home and family, after she was exiled from the outside world.

The following day, when Alice bade farewell to everything she had known since being born in the village, 'Liza was the last one to stand looking up at the northbound road and waving at the small figure sitting in the back of Tom Carter's small wagon as it rolled into the distance.

Chapter 20

In October, Edward Swarthye sent his regrets for not coming to see them, in a letter which accompanied a large bundle of haberdashery items; he informed them also that his business in London was keeping him occupied, which was more than could be said for some of the foreign traders around him. Thanks to his many friends, he was able to go about his business in the capital with relative ease, although the general feeling of the people varied enormously, with periods of calm alternating with uncertainty, when arrests were made. The most recent being the imprisonment of Bishop Fisher and some Observant Friars, from Greenwich.

(This news had already reached the Queen, Bella had informed 'Liza, and had caused her great anxiety about what would happen next. Bishop Fisher had been one of her greatest supporters.)

He also wrote about rumours that Thomas Cromwell, the King's adviser, was looking to close the smaller religious houses and throw the nuns and monks onto the streets, accusing them of all manner of dreadful acts, as well as treason, for not acknowledging the King as head of the English church. He did not add the rest of the gossip, which was the popular view that these closures were being enacted solely to enrich the King and Cromwell. Some things were best left unsaid.

He ended his letter by telling them he hoped to see them in the Spring, when the weather was better and travel was easier for everyone, but in the meantime the embroidered linen collars had been well received and this commission would continue; he was sending the money he owed her with John Carter, a man he trusted completely.

It was obvious to Hannah that the letter had been opened and carefully resealed, for Edward always placed a small piece of linen thread above his name which broke if the parchment was unrolled; the unseen message, the continuance of the smuggling of information to and from the Queen and her supporters – was safely conveyed, somewhat to Hannah's disappointment. As she had hoped that by now, another way would have been found and that she and 'Liza could move away from danger.

As night settled onto the day earlier and earlier, and the temperatures dropped, it became apparent that the walks in the park would have to be curtailed. Bella had the advantage of wearing thick, warm, fur lined cloaks with the hoods edged with more fur and had long fur lined leather boots to wear outside; and of course, her wool and linen day clothes were of a high quality.

'Liza was not so fortunate, despite wrapping a second shawl around the one wool cloak she owned, although it was thin, as it was not woven from thick wool in the first place. Her feet were now in leather shoes and oversized wooden clogs and her thick woollen stockings helped to keep her legs warm, but it was too cold to stop moving and sit down anywhere.

The park trees had lost most of their leaves, and their gaunt outlines now seemed rather threatening to the girls, looming over them and around them like black arms seeking to entrap them.

In spite of the worsening weather, there were several visitors to the Palace throughout October – some more welcome than others. Bella told 'Liza (on one of the last walks outside) that Father Bedyll had come to harangue the Queen once more with the threat of going into a convent, although he had tried to pretend that such a move was a natural one for such a devout woman.

Thomas Bedyll, a weasel-faced man of middle height was well known in London as a spy for Thomas Cromwell, so his presence at the Palace made several of the ladies and grooms uneasy, for his sharp eyes seemed to peer into every nook and cranny of life with Queen Katharine.

He was a monk, but the King's man, and therefore refused to acknowledge or address Katharine as Queen. In return, Katharine refused to tolerate him near her in the Chamber or Hall, while in the chapel, he was forced to give way to Father Athequa of course, who was the senior churchman. It was fortunate that Thomas Bedyll did not understand Spanish for he was the object of more insults and bad wishes than any man who had been there before! No one liked him, not even the bishop's servants, and it was a great relief to all when he left.

On All Hallows Eve, when Christians were asked to pray for the passage of souls still in Purgatory, Reverend White set off early in the morning and by Sext was halfway round the village, blessing each house and hovel; the holy water was carried by a succession of boys, chosen by him from the families he felt deserved the honour, and he had instigated a regular rota for the bell ringing to begin at Vespers and go on through the night. Most people were glad to just shut their doors at sunset and stay inside – just in case something untoward should happen, but not the young of the village.

Bella had sent word that she would be unable to see 'Liza, but that from the following week, Hannah was requested to come to the Palace, and she could then accompany Bella back to the house. The groom who recited the message was visibly relieved to have discharged his task, as he looked about him with a noticeable degree of contempt, for he turned quickly and ran back before Hannah could thank him.

The laundress's kitchen was a hive of activity: Liza who had been gathering several baskets of the last hips and sloes from the hedgerows over the previous week, was patiently tipping some of the hips into the bubbling pot on the fire; Mistress Munnings was anxious to make a double quantity of her renowned winter cough elixir.

Benet suffered more and more each winter with chesty coughs and the hip water mixed with honey afforded him some relief. The sloes could be made into wine later. Meanwhile, her mother and Charity Munnings were busy making soul cakes, ready for the evening.

Benet had fetched more frothy yeast (and extra honey) for the mammoth baking session. He had jumped the queue at Goodwife Bowyer's brewhouse and been roundly cat-called and jostled so much, that he nearly dropped the full pot, but fortunately, Rowland Langland had stepped in to shield him – and no one messed about with Rowland, whose muscles told of his hours in the smithy.

Benet would be going souling with 'Liza that evening, and little Grace Gilbert would go for the first time, accompanied by big sister Mary. They would collect soul cakes from all round the village houses and in return, promise to pray for whomever was nominated.

This year, Mistress Fauconer had given her friend some of the orange peel skins that had been left over from this fruit after it had been prepared for the Queen, and Hannah was busily slicing them into very small, narrow strips to be added to the cake mixture. Edward had sent more nutmeg and clove, as requested, and as an unexpected bonus, a screw of paper had revealed saffron. Such an expensive gift! Charity Munnings had raised her eyebrows when she saw the spice, but said nothing other than, "We will make a batch of cakes for ourselves with that; no good wasting it on the people round here for they won't appreciate its taste!"

This busy kitchen scene was being repeated in every home, and even in the kitchen of the Palace there was a similar flurry of activity, for there were always a large number of callers there, expecting a high standard of baking too. Bella had been asked to help with the carrying of the cakes to the room behind the dole window, for Lord Dymock knew that the Queen would be on her knees in the chapel all night, praying for who knows how many souls, and would stay there until the first mass on All Saints Day.

Mistress Fauconer had been told to give out the cakes and ask the recipients to pray for the King, Queen Anne and the Princess Elizabeth. Bella told 'Liza to pray for Queen Katharine and Princess Mary instead.

There was some good-natured squabbling between the many groups as they went up and down the village streets, for some had torches that lasted longer than others, and more than one group had to finish their evening dependent on the moon, but everyone returned home safely, thoroughly chilled, but very satisfied with the cakes they had gathered.

How much praying was done remained unknown, although as 'Liza and Benet joined Hannah and Charity in the warm sweet-smelling kitchen as usual, for the regular evening prayer, before they all retired for the night, once Charity had finished reciting, "O everlasting light whose brightness never darkens; look favourably on us Thy poor and sinful servants," she had added "and we pray for all those souls who remain in purgatory that they gain entry to Heaven and Your blessed presence, Amen."

It saved Benet worrying that he might have forgotten to pray for someone whose cake he had taken and eaten.

Chapter 21

When Hannah went to collect Isabella and accompany her to the laundry house, she was given a box by Lady Darrell – it contained some games; the Queen thought that playing chess would be a good way to pass the time and that 'Liza would enjoy it. She had already commissioned the set of pieces and a small board from William Gilbert, although it had been Thomas who had actually done the carving, especially after learning that it was to be a gift for Hannah and her daughter. There was also the game of 'Fox and Goose' and the promise of a backgammon set when Thomas had finished it. The guards examined everything in the box but failed to spot the message hidden in the false bottom of the chess board.

Bella took it out and handed it to 'Liza while pretending to show her the carving on the lid, and 'Liza was equally careful to keep it in her hand until she could go to her room. She hid it in her grandmother's shofar for the time being.

Sitting near the window, in the warm kitchen, they all listened as Bella explained the rules of 'Fox and Goose:' "So, if you land here on 'The Tavern' you will miss two goes, and here, if you land on the Maze, you can move forward to square 30." Benet was peering at the board, and Hannah had a sudden thought that Benet might be able to use her mother's eyeglasses and went off to get them.

"You have to land exactly on square 63 to win and if you don't have the right number to get there you miss your turn. D'Entendeis? Do you understand?"

Benet shook his head, and his bottom lip wobbled "I c c can't count that many," he told Bella.

Charity could not count that many at once either but would not admit it.

'Liza leaned forward, "You don't need to count to 63 at the same time Benet, just count the number you throw each time and then, depending on where you land, you move or not and don't worry, I'll help you."

His face lit up at this and then brightened even more when he was given the eyeglasses. Hannah warned him that he could only wear them when he was playing one of the games and when she or 'Liza gave them to him, for he had immediately got up and was wandering round the kitchen, whooping delightedly as he looked at various things, especially when he found a pan that had been carelessly hung and pointed this out to his mother.

“Just wemble it Benet! Don’t tell me, just do it!” his mother told him crossly, seeing this oversight as a criticism of her housekeeping, which in a way it was.

Hannah was more concerned that he cease his wandering around and sit down, and more importantly, that he should understand that the eyeglasses were precious and could not be taken outside the house where they were sure to be broken or lost, or taken by someone who thought it would be a fun thing to do to Benet.

The eyeglasses had been an inspired idea of Hannah’s, for while he was wearing them, Benet was very good at the games they played, especially ‘Fox and Goose’, which Bella brought with her the following week. In addition, he was given the important task of putting each game piece away carefully and Hannah made some little coloured bags for him to use so that the games’ pieces didn’t get mixed up.

For Bella, looking back on that autumn in Bugden, those visits to a poor home where she was welcomed as if she were a member of the family and shared in laughter and teasing and honey cakes, were some of the happiest times in her life. She felt loved and secure, except when she was carrying a message, although the passing of the messages had become relatively easy, for the guards had grown careless at the repetition of the weekly visits and made only cursory searches. The pomander was never, ever touched. Nevertheless, Hannah warned her not to become complacent, just one tiny slip and they could all be arrested.

Whatever the messages said and from whom, 'Liza never knew, and having pondered on it, she thought it best that she did not know; Bella could only tell her whatever the Queen decided to say openly, for she too never tried to look at what had been written. Bella presumed, from the little that was said out loud, that the messages had to do with the campaign of the Spanish Ambassador to obtain the Queen's release, for his name cropped up a number of times.

However, the Queen continued to feel disappointed that life did not seem to change for her in any way at all; Henry was appealing against his excommunication and by association the Pope's ruling that her marriage to him was valid. She was aware more than ever of being constantly watched, and her fear increased when Elizabeth Barton, the Holy Nun of Kent, and Fathers Bocking and Risby were publicly paraded and denounced.

Who would be next the Queen wondered?

As winter advanced stealthily towards them, they all felt the change and life seemed to become quieter; even the traffic on the Great North Road slackened off. Days were colder and shorter and washing became the drudge that it always was when you had to break the ice on the water in the buckets and the sting of the cold water on your hands and feet numbed them into nothingness.

There were plenty of other jobs that kept them occupied – vegetables to be put into the sand boxes ready for the very hard winter months, and meat and fish salted away; one pig had been slaughtered and 'Liza felt she had made enough brawn to feed the village. Every housewife had the same worry – would there be enough to last the winter? For in some years winter lasted well into what ought to have been spring.

While Bella continued to act as courier for the Queen and 'Liza and her mother continued in their clandestine operation to ensure that all messages sent or received were passed on as quickly as possible, for the villagers, life continued as it had always, and there were times when the villagers actually forgot that there was a Queen living among them.

With Ann Serle suffering ill health in her pregnancy and unable to work, John Serle had obtained work at the village forge, which lay along Hoo Baulk. Plough shares needed sharpening or renewing at this time of year, ready for the new ploughing season, and these required a lot of work by the skilled Forgemaster, John Burges and his apprentice Hugh, who were glad to pay a little money to John to make the trek on the other side of the village to the charcoal maker, William Coler.

He made the charcoal in the woods to the west and across from the Great Road and he also saw to the coppicing work which ensured the woods of all landowners, large and small, were managed for the best. An old man of few words, he was one of the few villagers who did not seem to mind working in the woods up Hobgoblin Lane which had a fearsome reputation, although 'Liza could never find out why this was.

When at home, William Coler lived alone up Tailleurs Lane and seemed to prefer his own company or that of the trees he tended, rather than that of people; nonetheless, he was a regular sight in the village with his old horse pulling a wagon piled with the wood and charcoal that everybody needed for their heating and cooking.

John Serle was away from his wife and children each day, working until long after sunset; and Hannah and Mistress Munnings worried about the state of the family. Sometimes they talked quietly about what might happen if Ann Serle continued to be so poorly and so, did their best to keep the children fed and clothed, as they always looked so dauncey. Hannah feared that at least one of the children would not see another year, she was so frail and wasted, and she had 'the cough'.

Bella, meanwhile, was becoming increasingly worried about the Queen, who spent more and more time praying and appeared to have lost a lot of her usual good spirits. The two household lords continually harassed her to accept her position as Princess Dowager, which she steadfastly refused to even acknowledge – for it would mean that she would disinherit her own daughter. The febrile atmosphere was dispiriting for everybody in the Tower and even made the villagers jumpy; and messages or no messages, Hannah had a growing feeling that the Queen was battling a lost cause.

"It is a great sadness that she has not seen the Princess Mary for more than two years now. Of course, she will do nothing to undermine her daughter's position, and that places them both in a dreadful position. Her own father, the King, treats her as less of a daughter than he does his bastard girl child," said Bella one afternoon when they were lingering over a chess game, which 'Liza had found that she liked to play; she relished the need to outthink her opponent and could not help but feel elated when she beat her.

"Can you imagine how that must feel? And the Princess Mary knows that her mother is suffering here. There has been talk again of the Princess being sent to Hatfield, to act as a servant for the baby Elizabeth, and the Queen fears that it is no rumour and will happen soon." Bella moved one of her pieces, and continued, "She has been told that the Princess is still unwell and yet the King has once again denied her permission to visit her daughter."

Bella sighed, "The only positive fact is that the King has fathered another girl child and not the son he so desperately wanted, so there are now two Princesses. In spite of what the king has been saying to everyone, that Princess Mary is no longer the

Princess Royal, she is in fact, next in line for the throne."

"I wonder what would have happened to the Princess Mary if it had been a boy," murmured 'Liza.

Bella shook her head, "Don't! Don't even think about it, I just thank God it was a girl – a son and heir would have caused so many more problems for Her Majesty and her daughter!"

When 'Liza repeated this information to her mother later that night, she asked if Hannah thought that the Queen got all her information from the messages that she received via them, or if someone else was keeping her in touch with what was happening at the King's court. It seemed to make sense that someone else was in contact with the Queen. Hannah shushed her, for even to talk about any of this was dangerous, and the mother in her felt guilty that she had exposed her daughter to enough possible danger of arrest as it was.

And so, the days passed in a mixture of routine drudgery for most, plus the weekly visits from Bella, whose conversation contained enough general information, not only to keep Mistress Munnings happy and the villagers in awe of the laundress, but helped to remind the villagers that a Royal Queen was sheltered in the Palace.

Chapter 22

Martinmas was the start of the Church's command to fast three times a week – to prepare their souls for the Mass of Christmas and the celebration of Christ's birth. 'Liza hated it, and Benet frequently broke it. Bella worried that the Queen would become very ill, she fasted so often in normal times, and she had already lost weight, requiring her clothes to be altered.

Reverend White did not seem to lose any weight, and worse, he continued to preach long sermons each Sunday, with an especially long one on the Feast Day of Saint Hugh of Lincoln, although he told them, on the Sunday following, that he had been disappointed with the number in the congregation on that feast day, and the churchwardens would be asking why there had been no attendance from any family not represented then. Charity merely told them, when asked, that given the run of poor weather they had suffered, she had too many back orders to fulfil, some of which had been for Master White, at the Palace. She had then walked away without waiting for any more dialogue with them.

Two Observant Friars came to the Palace. They were well received by the two courtiers, if not by the Queen. Their reputations as spies for Cromwell preceded them, thanks to the tales by the pedlars from London, and so, although Brother Lawne and Brother

Lyst were shown great courtesy and were treated with polite deference at all times, by the Palace inhabitants as well any villager they spoke to, even they could see that this was merely a front.

Everyone to whom they spoke, was polite but distant and professed to know nothing about any matters within the Palace or beyond the village's bounds. When asked directly, the villagers acknowledged Katharine to be 'the Queen' which both angered and worried the two men, who duly reported this to Cromwell; while their paymaster merely added this report to the many others on his desk, adding to his certainty that the King needed to do something about *Queen* Katharine at Bugden.

The last week in November seemed to be particularly hard on the Queen and she became snappish and difficult to please. Bella was glad of the sympathy she received from 'Liza and the others when she sat with them at their kitchen table. She told them of the week she had just suffered at the Palace, beginning with the day before the anniversary of the death of Queen Isabella, Katharine's mother, and which of course, had meant a day of prayers and a full requiem mass for the dead queen's soul, when the news had broken that the King had publicly demoted the Princess Mary, revoking both her title and position as heir presumptive.

Queen Katharine's distress forced her to take to her bed and Doctor de la Sa immediately ordered a potion to calm her nerves; this meant that John de Soto, and

Philip Greenacre, the Queen's apothecaries, had to ride into Huntingdun (with an escort of guards) to obtain the missing ingredient they needed, and replenish other supplies; for the Queen constantly suffered from a cough. Nightshade and rose, and pomegranate they had, but no barkberry bark, and in any case, this potion was to be made solely by de Soto and Philip Greenacre, for Doctor de la Sa did not trust anyone outside this tiny inner circle of the Queen's supporters at the Palace.

When the two girls next met, Bella had a great deal of news to tell her friends: the start of Advent meant that the Queen had embarked on an even more rigorous fasting regime, refusing all meat, eggs and cheese, so that she could show her utter devotion to God and then finally enjoy the celebration of Christ's birth.

She was convinced that her devotion to both God and the Church would be rewarded by political gains to her cause and that of the Princess Mary, and while she did not expect all her servants to do the same as her, she encouraged them to do so, telling them of the joys of denial and suffering for Jesus' sake and the great satisfaction of honouring his birth, while earning redemption from time in purgatory and a greater reward in Heaven.

Bella was finding all of this extremely hard to take and 'Liza sympathised with her. The Munnings family and their friends joined in the advent fast but with little conviction, especially when the weather was cold and the work hard, but their frequent failures resulting in warm food in their bellies, made the cold bearable.

For Bella, there was no chance that she could break the fasting when she was with the Queen in the Tower, and there were already dark shadows under her eyes, while the prominence of her nose showed that she had lost weight. If Bella had lost this much weight, thought 'Liza, the Queen must be really thin.

Bella drank some hot water (to which Hannah had added a little honey), closing her eyes in happiness, as the sweetness filled her mouth, before continuing, "Also, Her Majesty has had news that her goddaughter Katharine Willoughby has married the Duke of Suffolk. His first wife Mary was the sister of King Henry, you know, and she was a great friend of the Queen for many years. Her Majesty was devastated when Lady Mary died suddenly in the summer. Her Majesty is more than a little worried, for Donna Maria, the bride's mother, has not written to tell the Queen why the marriage has taken place now."

She took another sip, "Can you believe it? Katharine Willoughby is only our age, just 14 years old and now married to a man of 50!"

"Not unusual in aristocratic circles," observed Hannah, quietly.

"But think of it, a husband of 50!" said Bella, rolling her eyes at 'Liza who felt very glad that she was not a rich young heiress.

"A rich man is a rich man, and don't forget he was brother-in-law of the King, and is still his great friend," Hannah told them, "I believe this Duke was made her guardian after her own father died. She is wealthy and men being men, they are always greedy for more land and income."

The fire crackled and 'Liza bent down to put on more wood and give her friend a little time to compose herself, for her bottom lip was wobbling and she was swallowing back her tears. Even when the two girls started to talk about Christmas, Bella immediately said it would not be a very jolly time at the Palace. After all this depressing news, the Queen was less and less interested in enjoying life.

When the news of Princess Mary's final removal to Hatfield, to act as a servant to her half-sister, was brought to the village inns via the travellers from London, 'Liza presumed that this would immediately cancel any thought of enjoyable festivities at the Palace. There would be no Christmas revelry at the Palace.

What more misery would the Queen and her household have to endure? she wondered, as she settled to sleep that night.

Chapter 23

The King's Messenger clattered up the Great North Road, blowing his horn to clear the way, a common sight on this particular highway and few people bothered to watch him as he trotted northwards; if they had, they would have seen him swerve into the outer gatehouse and disappear from view. His reappearance was an hour or so later, on a fresh horse, and with his green uniform now freed from its accumulation of mud and dust, but now travelling south, and also went unremarked.

However, in the Queen's chambers, it was the cause of great anxiety as Lord Mountjoy, her chamberlain, informed the Queen that several lords, including the Duke of Suffolk, who had been personally tasked by the King, would be seeking an audience of the utmost importance with her in the forthcoming days, and then left her to worry and wonder over what this might mean for her future. Mistress Munnings wanted more details.

"Nothing more was said?"

Bella shook her head, and wriggled her toes nearer the fire, "The entire Palace is in uproar at having to find so many rooms for the lords and their retainers so quickly, and it appears that some of their servants will have to go to the Lion."

Charity Munnings stood up. "I think I need to go to the Palace and speak with Mistress Fauconer –

there may be a need for fresh linen, and it is difficult to wash and dry a lot of linen at short notice at this time of year."

"What about the guards?" 'Liza called after her, "won't they find it odd if you go round without taking anything with you?"

Charity paused and looked back, "Hmm, maybe I will take the trolley then, I'll cover it over with the leather and they'll not stop me. If they do, I'll report them to Master White; I can just see him rushing around in a panic. So, he won't be at all pleased if he is summoned to the outer gatehouse." She smiled at the thought.

Unfortunately, Mistress Fauconer could not add anything to what Bella had already told them. Lord Mountjoy had gone at once to his office, to write a reply for the messenger to take back to London, while she had been directed to take a tray of meats and bread to the inner gatehouse, where the messenger was waiting to eat, and then was simply given his outer coat to brush and clean as best she could. She had been summarily dismissed by the sergeant there too.

It did not stop Charity from discussing what it might mean with all her friends and cronies, over the next few days, but everyone agreed that whatever it was, it did not bode well for the Queen. Michael Longland told anyone who would listen, that if anything untoward happened, he would organise the villagers on the Queen's behalf. After that, there was nothing more they could do except wait for whatever was coming up the road towards them all.

The morning of Katharine's birthday passed like any other, but the celebrations in the Palace were muted. Bella had embroidered a handkerchief with pomegranates and roses, with a little help from Hannah, and the Queen was very touched by this thoughtful gift. Some wine was drunk and then they all gathered together in the Great Chamber, where the fire was roaring, which created some warmth in the bleak room, and settled down to play some games. The light was too poor for sewing.

Father Abell, the Queen's English chaplain went out to collect some candles for the chapel – there was to be a special mass said for Katharine – and was halted temporarily at the sight of several men at arms and others trotting into the inner courtyard and clattering across the bridge. Startled, he barely had time to think about what this meant before he was seized by two guards and taken straight into the outer gatehouse. There was no time to warn the Queen.

More men at arms and servants with pack horses streamed in, but the noise had now become too great to ignore. Lady Darrell opened the outer door of the chamber and took in the scene at once. On the street, the last of the riders passed by the smithy and Michael Longland watched through narrowed eyes. He was not daunted by their numbers, for he could rouse twice as many men if need be. He began to remove his leather apron and set off around the village to prepare the men to defend the Queen.

Meantime, forewarned by Lady Darrell, the Queen had already risen from her chair in the Great Chamber, and now took herself off to her rooms in the Tower. Later, Bella told them, as she had risen to her feet, she had clapped her hand to gain their attention and said that as she had no idea what this visit meant for her or any of them, she wanted them to know that she was forever grateful for their company and loyalty and would remember them all in her prayers, then looking at each of them she had said, "I am ready to die; I am the King's true wife and were he to command me to walk into the fire I would do so, in honour of his wish as husband and king. I hope for the best outcome but fear the worst."

In the Palace, the assembled lords had refreshed themselves and spoken for some time with Lord Mountjoy, and then they issued a series of orders. All the Queen's under servants, except for the ladies and maids with her in the Tower rooms, were to leave the Palace immediately, there were to be no excuses and the guards were not interested in their pleas about having business to complete in the village, or that they worked directly for the Queen. Dismissed on the spot, and forced to leave in the middle of December, they had little except the clothes they were wearing.

On the orders of Lord Mountjoy, Kitchen Agnes swept through their dormitory, gathering everything she could, dumping it all in one large heap in the outer courtyard for them to sort through. It was all she was permitted to do. The Palace servants, who owed their service to the Bishop, were safe – but for how long?

As the newly dismissed men and women streamed out of the Palace, many of them weeping and cursing, they were offered beds and food by the villagers who had been summoned by Michael and who had gathered on the street. It was not an auspicious start to the visit. Charity took in a couple of the lesser maids, who were glad to be given some covers and allowed to sleep in the small barn after a bowl of barley broth, before leaving the next morning.

Benet could not understand why any of it was happening and kept asking his mother what it meant, but neither Hannah nor his mother could give him a satisfactory answer. He huddled near the fire, cuddling the kitchen cat until it grew tired of being constrained and scrambled its way off his lap.

Meanwhile, Michael organised a rota of boys to watch the gatehouse.

That first morning in the Great Chamber – where Katharine had agreed to see the visitors later (for she wanted there to be witnesses to whatever was about to unfold) the drama began. Mistress Fauconer stood off in one corner, ready to summon whoever or whatever might be needed by the important men at the far end of the room. She would never forget what happened.

The Queen was seated in a large, red upholstered chair and her ladies and all the maids, surrounded her, some standing, others sitting. Embroidery frames were in all hands except the Queen's, hers lay clasped lightly together on her lap. It was a perfectly set stage. She calmly watched as the lords approach her.

They bowed as one, sweeping off their bejewelled velvet hats and bending low, then straightening up and forming a small cluster around the Duke of Suffolk. The Queen nodded to each man, "My lords Suffolk, Somerset, Sussex, Winchester, I greet you all. There is wine if you need it," and she indicated a small table near the fire.

The Duke of Suffolk who was wishing himself anywhere else but here, cleared his throat and stepped forward, "Your Royal Highness," he got no further for the Queen raised her hand.

"Who is it you wish to speak to?" she queried.

If Charles Brandon had ever thought his task would be easy, this one question confirmed just how hard life for him, and the other commissioners, had suddenly become.

"Your Royal Highness," he repeated testily, "you are aware that the title of Queen is no longer yours, by decree of the King, Parliament and the Church, and therefore I address you as Her Royal Highness the Princess Dowager; this title having been granted to you by His Majesty in recognition of your status as a princess of Spain and the many years you spent in a marriage which is now recognised as no longer valid." He paused as a small trickle of sweat found an escape route down his face from under his cap.

The Queen's eyes narrowed at this speech, and then she suddenly rose from her seat, summoning every ounce of her courage and a lifetime of training, she seemed suddenly to grow taller, "I am Katharine, the true wife of King Henry and Queen of England and I will be hewn into pieces before I will accept any other title; as long as I live I will call myself Queen of England," she spoke loudly and clearly, then swept regally from the room followed by her ladies, leaving the men open mouthed – and furious.

Chapter 24

The bells had rung for Sext and the visitors had been given a small meal, before they all met again, as before, in the Great Chamber. The fire was small, and the room had already grown cold, so all of them sent for their cloaks, as they held a meeting to plan how they would approach the Queen once more with the King's demands. Charles Brandon steeled himself for the task personally allotted him, by the King, which he freely confessed he found difficult and distasteful.

The lengthy debate between the lords started off low key, but soon they were at loggerheads. "Enough time has been wasted," said the Duke of Somerset, "the Princess Dowager will never accept her new position, so best to just tell her what will happen to her, regardless of whether she agrees with it or not."

William Paulet, the Marquis of Winchester agreed, "Seymour is right. That obstinate woman will never agree to anything the King asks or orders. She forgets her place, she is merely a woman in his kingdom. Take her from here and lock her up in Somersham. With any luck the foul air there will do the King's work for him," he snarled, before adding, "then we can all go home and celebrate Christmas in comfort."

"Such obduracy can only be beaten out of her, and we don't have permission to do that. There's nothing to be done but convey her by force to Somersham," agreed Seymour.

Henry Radclyffe, the Duke of Sussex protested that carting her off by force would damn Henry in the eyes of all the world and that would be the last thing he would want, given that he prided himself on being viewed by all as a chivalrous ruler.

Charles Brandon, whose first wife had been a lifelong friend of the Queen, and who had, as a consequence of this, himself been part of her circle for many years, knew that Henry's reputation both in the country and abroad, would suffer severely if they were to simply remove her without her consent, shook his head, telling them all that they needed to accomplish this with as little aggravation as possible. Lastly, he informed them, that the King had advised him that force was the last and least desired option. Privately he could see no way of conveying her to Somersham peaceably, however he was not about to voice that opinion.

Divided in method, if not in purpose, they asked to see the Queen again and were shown into the Great Hall, where Katharine arrived accompanied by all her ladies. She went on to the attack at once, processing to the oriel window and turning abruptly to face them.

Ignoring the other three lords she spoke directly to Charles Brandon, "I am surprised to see you here my lord Suffolk, so soon after your unexpected wedding to my dear goddaughter. How does Katharine?"

This was unexpected, and good manners forced the Duke to reply through gritted teeth: "Extremely well and,"

Queen Katharine interrupted him, "I still grieve the death of my dear friend, your beloved first wife Mary – not very many months since" and she bowed her head, her lips moving silently, before crossing herself.

Charles Brandon, who had truly loved his first wife, the King's sister, bowed his head at this, as the other lords behind him began to murmur quietly about time being wasted. Then lifting his gaze to hers he said with sincerity, "Your sympathy is of great comfort to me, Madam, but,"

The Queen had not finished with him, however, and continued, "I was more than surprised to learn that Katharine was to be wed at such a young age, but I realise you were able to convince Lady Willoughby that, as an honourable man, you would take the greatest care of her daughter – otherwise she would never have assented to the match."

The unmistakeable emphasis on 'honourable' caused the Duke more than a pang of remorse. It was common knowledge on the streets of London that Lady Willoughby, the former Donna Maria de Salvinas, and favourite lady in waiting of the Queen for many, many years, was anxious to return to serve Katharine once more, following the death of her husband, and her daughter's recent marriage. A request which had been swiftly refused by King Henry.

The other three decided that this had gone on for too long and Somerset tapped his foot in annoyance, while looking threateningly at the Queen. Paulet began to clear his throat.

Katharine ignored them both.

The Queen watched Charles Brandon's face carefully, "Of course, we all know how important it is for so young a girl to have the best possible husband to honour and protect and care for her. Marriage requires great love and forbearance by both parties, as we both know."

In the difficult silence that followed, the fire crackled and popped. The commissioners shuffled their feet uneasily, while willing Charles Brandon to put an end to this uncomfortable this diversion to their mission.

The Duke had nodded at this sentiment, but anxious to close the subject, he said loudly, "Just so, and you must know that I will always take great care of my wife and her happiness will be of the first consideration to me. Now I MUST speak to you of other matters."

He had avoided addressing her by title and felt he could now proceed to tell her, that the King had graciously decided that if she did not wish to enter a nunnery – which would be by far the best option for such a pious lady, she was to be moved to the Bishop of Lincoln's establishment at Somersham, and that he and the other lords were there to facilitate that move.

"Somersham?" came the incredulous voice of Lady Darrell, "you are proposing to move the Queen to that pestilential rat hole of a place in the fens? You are perhaps unaware of her poor health? Her doctor will never agree to her going anywhere so damp and injurious to her lungs!"

The Queen frowned severely at the Duke and rebuked him by saying, "God never called me to a nunnery."

Lord Paulet stepped forward, impatient to have done with all of this talk, "In the event of refusing to enter a nunnery, the Princess Dowager,"and he laid a heavy emphasis on the title, "will be moved forthwith to Somersham and she will direct all of you to that end," he nodded at all the ladies in turn, then glanced at the walls, "you may of course take any tapestries or other furnishings that are personal to you. I should add of course that all your servants have already been instructed to address you as 'your Royal Highness' and not doing so renders them liable to imprisonment in the Tower at the King's pleasure," and he fixed them all with a piercing stare.

The ladies started to protest at this and mutter to each other about the implied threat, their faces betraying how horrified they felt, but the Queen merely stood and speaking slowly and clearly said to the men, "You must bind me with ropes and violently enforce me there. I would rather be hewn in pieces. I am the Queen and will not accept being Princess Dowager. There is nothing further to say."

With that she swept out of the room, hurriedly followed by her ladies.

Chapter 25

Charles Brandon asked to see the Queen alone in the Great Chamber, after Compline, hoping that he might be able to avoid further argument and the use of force by using their old friendship and past shared history to convince her of the futility of resistance to the King's order. He could see no easy way through the current impasse, unless he could use his personal friendship to make her agree to leave Bugden peacefully.

Leaving the other lords to their evening meal, he slipped away.

Queen Katharine swept into the chamber, accompanied by Lady Darrell and Bella who both sat away from the two protagonists near the door. Queen Katharine had dressed in her best scarlet silk overdress, and was wearing several jewels, for she knew that to be a Queen, you had to both feel and look like one.

After seating themselves either side of the fireplace, Katharine told the Duke of Suffolk that he should save himself from arguing with her, for she would never accept that her marriage was unlawful and never withdraw her appeal to the Pope. "God, in whom all my hopes are concentrated will not abandon me in this cause, in which justice is so clearly with me."

She further told him that as the King himself had been the first to appeal to the Pope about their marriage status, then it was only right and fair that she should appeal to him also, and that they both should await the full outcome of the Papal findings. Besides, she told him, the King's refusal to acknowledge the validity of her marriage was contrary to God's own law and imperilled the King's very soul. She would never agree to be part of that. "I'll not damn a soul for anything. I pray for the King daily."

Charles Brandon shook his head from time to time at this outpouring, and then quietly told her that her obstinacy would leave him with no option but to carry her to Somersham by force, and that all the other commissioners were in full agreement on this. In addition, the questioning of her servants would begin the following morning and they would be asked to swear an oath that the king's marriage to Queen Anne was valid, and that he was the Head of the Church in England, and lastly, that her own title was that of Princess Dowager,

Katharine looked at him, saying quietly, "I will not tolerate any in my household who take such an oath or who agree to address me as Princess Dowager. Anyone who does so is a guard of yours and not a servant of mine. Why, I would rather sleep in my clothes and lock my door myself than surround myself by such as those that you approve of."

Lady Darrell shook her head at this; and as if she could see her, the Queen asked her to fetch some wine for her and the Duke. Bella then concentrated on the low conversation that took place – because she heard her name mentioned.

The Queen leaned forward slightly and told Charles Brandon that her maid, Bella, who was the same age as his wife, was her goddaughter, just as his new wife was her goddaughter. However, Bella was an orphan, and unlike his wife, without friends or any support other than the Queen herself, for she had lived her whole life with her at court. "I made a promise to her mother as she lay dying that I would take care of her daughter. A deathbed promise, made before God, Charles."

The Duke shifted uneasily in his chair.

"I am asking you, therefore, to ensure that she remains with me – perhaps you would interrogate her yourself, and your decision would be made without reference to the other commissioners," she paused and looked straight at him, "I am asking you this in the name of Mary your first wife, and my friend, who would never hurt an innocent such as Isabella."

Charles Brandon was very tired, and his head was aching, moreover he found himself struggling with his duty, his emotions and his shared history with the Queen. He was already totally sick of this whole business and was facing the very real prospect of having to take the woman, against her will, to some wretched place in the Fens. On balance, what she was asking of him seemed a very little thing to do for her.

Sighing, he merely nodded his agreement at her and told her to have Isabella present herself to him in the chapel at Prime the next morning, where he would speak with her – but he added, he would make no promises.

The Queen had to be content with that, and murmured, "Thank you, my lord. I know that I can rely on your honour to see that no innocent child suffers unduly." She left, with Bella scuttling behind her, her mind reeling with the implication of all that she had just heard.

Charles Brandon made his way to the steward's office to check that all the arrangements for questioning the Queen's servants had been put in place. He met with a very short, testy response and was asked to leave so that the steward could deal with several other pressing matters, brought about by this visit.

In fact, Richard White was almost beyond himself with the stress of housing and feeding, the lords and their retainers at such short notice and was forced, reluctantly, to demand the best rooms at the Lion to ease the accommodation crisis.

Also, he was having to deal with the inevitable clashes between the Bishop's servants and those of the lords, who seemed to think that they were too important to be relegated to the servants' hall for their meals.

In addition, and with no notice, he had been told to provide food and bedding for Father Abell, one of the

Queen's confessors, who it appears, had been locked in the outer gatehouse immediately after the lords had arrived, for, he was told with a touch of impatience, they had orders to send him straight to the Tower in London.

As if his life could not get any worse, he was frequently called to various places within the Palace grounds, just to deal with unfortunate problems arising from the behaviour of the London servants who made free with the female servants; in fact, he had only just returned from a noisy showdown with Lord Seymour.

So fraught had relations become that before retiring to bed, the steward put pen to paper and sent a report of all of these various mishaps and his efforts to resolve them, to his master the Bishop of Lincoln.

Bugden Palace was an unhappy place to be whether you were a visitor or a resident.

Chapter 26

The interrogation of Bella was brief and to the point. She was told that she must refer to the Queen as Princess Dowager and always address her as Your Royal Highness; apart from that she could go to the devil she was told and dismissed. She returned to stay with the Queen in her rooms in the Tower, relieved and upset in equal measure, for she knew that nothing in the Queen's life was certain any longer, and if a Queen could be used so harshly, what chance an orphan girl? She joined the Queen in waiting anxiously for the next crisis to unfold.

Others were not as fortunate as Bella. Most of her ladies and their maids said they could not take an oath to acknowledge Katharine as Princess, as to do so would force them to commit perjury. They had been told this by Father Abell and Father Barker – another reason for the removal of these English chaplains as quickly as possible.

"You must acknowledge Queen Anne as the lawful spouse of the King and agree also that the King is head of the church, in England," Paulet told the ladies, when they presented themselves to him, one at a time, the following day.

Dorothy Wheeler refused outright – a matter of conscience she said. Sisters Marjory and Elizabeth Otwell said that what was being asked of them risked them imperilling their immortal souls, while Emma

Browne and Blanche Twyford said they had no intention of committing perjury. The other two Elizabeths (Fyne and Lawrence) refused to believe that the King would ask them to do anything so wrong and betray all honour and refused point blank to repudiate the Queen in any way.

They were all dismissed instantly and given two hours to collect their personal belongings and leave the Palace. They were allowed to send messengers to their various families, asking for help to facilitate their leaving the Queen, but would have to stay locked in the dormitory in the outer courtyard until they left the following morning - with Lord Dymock who said, as Almoner, it was his duty to escort them all safely to London.

Elizabeth Darrell, whose father had once been Queen Katharine's chamberlain, wrestled with her conscience, but took the oaths as required, confessing later to Father de Athequa that God would see that her service to the Queen was of greater importance that her sworn oath, while privately adding that she had no intention of calling her Princess Dowager. The priest duly absolved her of any sin.

Francisco Phelippes, the Queen's maitre de salles, refused to take the oath and left as far as the White Horse, where he took a room to wait until the commissioners had left the Palace. Anthony Rocke, and Bastian Hennycock left with Lord Mountjoy, who had thankfully resigned the previous evening, as her chamberlain.

There was a slight pause after dinner while goodbyes were said, and tears were shed. The Queen regretted that she had very little to give them in token of their service to her but said the God would know how honourable and true they were. Later, the Queen summoned Lord Winchester to see her and informed him that whatever the result of his interrogation of Father de Athequa, she had never confessed in English and knew not how to do so – she only knew the Spanish way. To send him away would deny her the right of confession, and after a little debate amongst themselves, the commissioners informed the Dominican, as well as Doctor de la Sa and the two apothecaries, that they would be allowed to stay with the Queen for the foreseeable future, although this was not to be taken as an exoneration for not taking the oath.

The Palace suddenly went very quiet.

Mistress Fauconer took the Queen her dinner that evening, having first seen to the commissioners who were eating with Richard White. They were discussing the removal of the Queen and the imminent arrival the next day of the wagons which would take the Queen's personal belongings, clothing, furnishings and other pieces to Somersham with her.

The steward interrupted them, "And now that her ladies are no longer here, who is going to pack up all of her necessities?"

There was a silence. Their high-handed dismissal of the Queen's ladies in waiting had left them with a completely unforeseen difficulty. A message to the ladies in the dormitory asking them to return to do this task was met with a total refusal, and the message, 'We are no longer the ladies of the Queen and as such we are unable to help'.

Lord Winchester put his head in his hands, "Where does my lord Paulet think he could quickly find careful and honest hands to do the packing?" he asked.

For a brief moment, Charles Brandon felt a bubble of laughter in his chest, but he swallowed it down and looked at the Bishop's Steward and raised his eyebrows.

Richard White rose to the occasion. "If you will excuse me my lords, I think I may be able to help. There are some women in the village who are known and trusted by me and have always served the Bishop well. I am sure that I can presume on them to aid us in this matter. There may be the question of some payment for their time?"

Lord Somerset sighed, "Do what you can, White; I will give you a specific amount and you can negotiate whatever pay you want. I am sure ALL the money will be spent by you or whomever." He tossed a small bag of coins across the table.

Richard White gave a short bow of his head and scooped up the bag before any objections could be made. He went straight to his estate office and sent for the laundress.

Chapter 27

The following morning, as Bella and Elizabeth Darrell helped the Queen to dress, Hannah and her daughter, and Benet and his mother assembled in the Tower entrance with Mistress Fauconer. They were given instructions about packing the Queen's clothes and belongings in the trunks that would be arriving that morning with the wagons and told that any theft of the Queen's property would be treated with the harshest penalty.

Charity Munnings drew herself up at that and told the steward that she was an honest woman and so were those with her. He acknowledged this and said that on completion of this task, they would be paid a generous sum. (He had already deducted his own commission of course).

The three women and Benet slowly ascended the Tower staircase and entered the Queen's apartment. The panelled walls and heavy moulded beams of the ceiling made 'Liza feel small and insignificant, while Benet stood riveted to the spot. On one of the bosses of the beams was a wonderful carving of a thrush and Benet spotted it immediately. He gazed at it then pointed it out to 'Liza, urging her to come and 'look at the throstle.'

But 'Liza's eyes were taken with the richness of the tapestries hanging from the walls - the vivid scenes of the labours of Hercules and Jason and the

Argonauts told their stories in wonderful pictures. The needlework was exquisite, and she wondered who had stitched them.

"Those are the Queen's favourite stories," came a voice which 'Liza recognised as Bella's.

She spun around and looked at her friend with some alarm. Bella's face was pale and sickly, and her eyes were ringed by dark shadows; the strain of the last few days plain to see. If her friend looked so ill, 'Liza paused to wonder about the Queen.

"Her Majesty is in the chapel and refuses to leave while this is happening. Lady Darrell and I are here to help you. We will bring out the Queen's clothes and fold them, and then you will place them in the trunks. After that, all of her possessions must be carefully packed and last of all her bed hangings and her bed linen." Bella recited the plan but had scarcely reached the end before tears began to roll down her cheeks.

'Liza reached out and hugged her close, it was all she could think to do, and she felt her friend crumple in her arms as she whispered, "I have been so frightened 'Liza. I can stay with the Queen now through God's good grace, but I might have been turned out on the streets like the others – and I, and I, have nowhere to go."

She began to cry softly as 'Liza patted her shoulder, "The Queen, oh the Queen, she is so distressed, I fear for her sanity, she kneels and prays or sits and says not a word, and every time she has returned from speaking with them, she has been trembling so much. She is so brave."

Hannah came forward and put her arms round both of them. Lady Darrell watched from the door of the Queen's bedroom, her face showing her concern and distress at the sorrowful scene and Benet sniffed loudly.

At length, Bella broke away saying, "I must be strong for her sake. So, where shall we start?"

By the time the wagons arrived mid-morning and the empty trunks had been unloaded and brought up into the Tower, the pile of clothes was ready: befurred nightgowns, lawn chemises, caps and stammels, bejewelled bodices, girdles, several velvet and woollen outer gowns, a scarlet Amsterdam woollen cloak, a blue cloak and several hoods. 'Liza had never seen so many clothes and could not help but stroke the furs and velvets. She was told this was nothing compared to the Queen's wardrobe when she had been with the court. Her wardrobe then had consisted of hundreds of items.

Benet was standing on a chair and carefully unhooking the tapestry from its wooden pole. It was very heavy, and his mother and Hannah anxiously held the folds of wool as it came down. Hannah was actually more concerned about Benet than the tapestry.

Trunks began to fill up, and the women and Benet stopped when Kitchen Agnes appeared with some bread and cheese and a jug of ale. Benet needed the jakes and asked where to go. Bella showed him the garderobe in the tower and left him to find his own way back. He was amazed at the structure and began to tell his mother about it, while the others were still eating.

"Not now Benet!" she admonished, embarrassed by his lack of tact.

The heavy trunks were taken to the waiting wagons by some of the Bishop's servants and Thomas Payne and Will Style, who were part of Father de Athequa's retinue, who had taken the oath and been allowed to remain. Summoned to act as porters, they complained all the way down the staircase and at one point as Thomas was almost flattened when Will's grip slipped, a great deal of swearing was clearly heard by the packers upstairs.

By the middle of the afternoon, the Queen's litter had arrived in preparation for her leaving the Palace and the wagons were half full. Richard White came to see them, nodding his approval at the progress made; he was accompanied by Thomas Longland who had taken it upon himself, as a member of the Bishop's family, to also check what was happening.

On top of the table, next to the folded table runner, lay a blue velvet purse. Intricate gold bead and stitch work caused the blue and gold to complement each other so wonderfully that your eye became almost dazzled. After the two men had left, Bella moved across to Hannah.

"That man with the steward, I saw him! He took the Queen's purse!" she whispered to her friends indignantly, her eyes round with the shock of seeing such a brazen theft.

Hannah placed her arm on the girl's, "He is an important man in the village, and the Bishop's cousin - are you sure?"

"He is a thief!" spat Bella.

"Ssh," Hannah warned her, and thought for a moment, "If we tell the steward he will simply accuse one of us of taking it."

"But I will tell him I saw that man take the purse!"

Hannah shook her head, "And when he accuses Thomas Longland, what do you think that man will say? And which of us will be believed by the Steward? A relative of the Bishop, and a man! Of course, it will be his word that will count, and we will suffer because we are women, and of no account."

Bella shook her head, "It is not enough to do all this to her, they have also to steal from the Queen." She shook her head in disbelief and slumped onto the floor.

The steward sent Kitchen Agnes to tell the women to go but return the next morning, to finish their work by dismantling the bedchamber after the Queen had left. They must be finished by Sext he told them and meeting Charity and Hannah at the foot of the stairs, he handed them each a small bag of coins. Hannah debated whether to throw them back at him but thought better of it; she needed money if she was ever to return to London with 'Liza.

Upon being dismissed, Charity left the gatehouse and went straight to the smithy to speak to Michael; and they all noticed the satisfied smile on her face when she returned to the house. She waited until they were eating supper in the warmth of the kitchen, feeling tired and worn out after their day, before telling them that Michael had sworn to prevent the removal of the Queen, no matter what the cost.

"The King may think he can break the Queen's resolve, but he is wrong, moreover, those henchmen of his won't find it easy to take our Queen from us." She nodded at them, "I told Michael about tomorrow's events and by the end of this evening, the whole village will know as well. They have ignored us at their peril; now we all need to get a good night's sleep! Tomorrow will be a long day I think."

Chapter 28

On the last morning of the commissioners' planned stay, as the Queen sat in the Great Chamber accompanied only by Lady Darrell and Bella, the Duke of Suffolk rose and directed her and her ladies to dress for travel. She would be leaving for Somersham almost immediately, her litter was ready for her, and the village women would be coming to pack up her bedchamber as soon as she had left it. She stared at him coldly and then at each of the lords before rising from her chair.

She walked slowly and with great dignity to the door of the chamber and then turned, "I am the Queen of England and the King's true wife!" she shouted at them, and then whisked herself and the other two through the doorway. Immediately, the three of them fled up the tower staircase and into the now empty outer chamber. The door slammed shut and was locked from the inside.

Realising that he had been tricked, the Duke ran after her shouting at her to stop, but he was too late. He was forced to continue to harangue her by shouting through the keyhole, until the Queen replied just once that he would have to break down the door and carry her by force away from the Palace.

Meanwhile, outside the gatehouse, a mass of villagers, quickly gathered by Michael, had assembled in silence. They made no reply to the guards' taunts and jeers. Their only arms were their billhooks, scythes and other equipment, which they held before them like weapons, but they made no attempt to engage with the guards. Their silence however proved to be unnerving, and the guards were very relieved when their sergeant appeared followed by Lords Somerset and Suffolk.

For several minutes the two lords ordered, threatened, shouted, and finally implored them all to leave and get about their day's business. The villagers made no reply. A small convoy of wagons and drays were now gathered on the road at the northern end of the crowd, resigned to waiting for the large crowd to clear. At the smithy, a similar line of wagons was growing longer.Their drivers had drifted near to the gatehouse and had been told about the attempt to remove the Queen; their numbers swelled the crowd gathered there.

After a hurried conference of all the lords together,Edward Seymour stepped out and asked the villagers to allow them to leave the Palace, with no harm or fault to themselves or the rest of the villagers; at this, Michael stepped forward and calmly informed Lord Somerset that he and the rest of the lords and their servants were free to leave at any time, but the Queen stayed here.

Faced with the prospect of forcibly dragging the Queen into the litter, and quite possibly having to tie her into it to prevent her from escaping back into the Palace, and then fighting their way through or over the assembled villagers, witnessed by the drivers and merchants on the road, which action could easily lead to a riot, Edward Seymour decided to quit the contest.

He strode back into the inner courtyard, curtly told everyone assembled there that they would be leaving – without the Queen and ordered them to get ready. He would not be responsible for any loss of life here, not that the death of a few villagers bothered him, but the lords or their retainers might get badly hurt, and news of what happened here would spread quickly around the country and capital and reflect badly on the King. The others agreed with him.

Charles Brandon had already had enough of the whole business; someone else could take her to Somersham he decided. The dismissal of most of her servants would cause her life to be less than comfortable and he would send a couple of women from his own household to keep an eye on things for him. He told his men to mount and leave the wagons behind. Unpacking them was not his worry; he ordered the litter to be sent out first so that the villagers could see it was empty and then they would disperse.

Once the villagers saw that the Queen was not going to be taken away against her will, Michael ordered the villagers to go back to work. He stayed behind with a few men but only to make sure that all the incomers left and sent a couple of others to check on the men who had been staying in the Lion.

The cavalcade of men and horses, guarding an empty litter, trotted out and turned south for London, and with the road clear, the drivers and waggoners made haste to get back into their routine and proceed north or south to make up for lost time.

'Liza and her mother, with Charity who had been waiting at the roadside opposite the gatehouse, now entered the courtyard and were directed to return all the Queen's belongings to their original places, while the steward in a thoroughly bad temper stomped off to his office, to write another letter to the Bishop.

Almost unnoticed in the melee, Francisco Phelippes slipped back into the Palace, and sent a message to the Queen that he was at her service once more. Bella unlocked the door for her friends and together, with Lady Darrell they all began to put things back into their place.

The Queen spent the day on her knees on her prie-de-dieu, giving thanks that the Lord had spared her from certain death at the place called Somersham.

Thus ended the first attempt to remove the Queen from Bugden Palace.

Chapter 29

At the end of that tumultuous day and the departure that never happened, Bella slipped across the road and around the back of the laundress's house. She came to bring them the Queen's thanks for her rescue, knowing that Charity would be able to tell the villagers on her behalf.

"I cannot stay for long; the Queen is very tired."

"You look absolutely done in yourself," remarked Charity, "you're not leaving here until you've eaten a bowl of porridge. I don't care about the Advent fast, just tell that priest that you need all your strength to care for the Queen!"

She ladled a bowlful out and smothered it in honey, and after a brief hesitation, Bella accepted it and began to spoon it into her mouth, telling them all that the Queen's biggest fear now was that she would be poisoned.

"She has said she will no longer eat any meals prepared for her by the Bishop's servants. And so, Lady Darrell and I must prepare and cook for her in the outer room," Bella gave a huge sigh, "I know very little about cooking."

Charity was about to protest that her friend the housekeeper – or any one of the servants under her direction, would never, ever, do anything to hurt the Queen, but on reflection, acknowledged that someone could slip into the kitchen and add a little drop of this or that to the Queen's food.

Hannah had picked upon the practicalities of the situation, "You must not worry, Bella, for we will help you and give you food from time to time, although it will not be of the type that the Queen is used to; but it will be perfectly safe to eat."

"I'll show you how to do things and Mistress Munnings will ask Mistress Fauconer to give you some small pans and a skillet." 'Liza added, "We can give you some herbs and things, but best to ask Kitchen Agnes to give you anything straight from her hand to yours."

Hannah nodded. "And always go with Kitchen Agnes and see the water drawn from the pump," added Charity, ladling more porridge into the now empty bowl.

Benet then spoke, "I, I, w, w, w will help you. I'll bring things to you and you'll kn, kn, know it is safe to eat." He smiled, anxious to reassure this foreign girl of whom he had grown very fond.

Bella looked at them all and whispered her thanks, "I was not sure I could do this, but with your help I can. Te mantendre en mis oraciones cada noche," she paused then in English repeated, "I will keep you in my prayers each night." She scooped out the last of the porridge and licked her lips. "The Queen continues to fast so much, she will not notice what she is given to eat. Still," she heaved a sigh, "this will be hard on us all."

"Not much of a Christmas celebration for any of you either, but you must come here, and eat something with us," Charity told her as she took away the empty bowl.

On Christmas Eve it was the tradition to hang holly and ivy in the house and Benet retrieved the kissing bough frame from the small barn and decorated it with bay and mistletoe. 'Liza hoped that Thomas would not come round to the house too often!

As usual, a cup of spiced ale in their hands, they gathered around the fire and the adults told ghost stories. Benet leaned further and further into 'Liza until she put her arm round him, hugging him more tightly when the scariest bits caused him to shrink into her.

While Charity relished the old stories from her youth – Black Shuck the hell hound that roamed the fen was a particular favourite, she found a new twist on the story each Christmas, while the headless horseman was another one that she had learned as a child; and not to be outdone, Hannah told of the Santa Compana, the candle carrying ghosts who processed around, and the bell of La Velilla whose tolling was done by unseen hands. The Murcian screaming ghost caused even Charity to start up when a beam above her creaked in the rising wind, and at that point she declared it was time for sleep!

Benet went to the privy with his mother as escort that night.

Christmas Day followed its usual routine – there were three masses to attend, and a frantic search for the tapers which had to be held by every person in church (no smelly tallow candles would be tolerated), inadvertently exposed a mouse nest in the corner of the hall. Charity was scandalised and told Benet to immediately fetch one of the cats from the barn.

'Liza loved the carols, her favourite being 'Angels from the Realms of Glory' while Benet sang lustily, 'Ding Dong merrily on High' although the best part of the day for them all was dinner, which they consumed with gusto.

As she ate her suet pie, which contained the thirteen plums to represent Jesus and the Apostles, she asked Hannah to save a piece with at least one plum in it for Bella, and Charity immediately removed the remains of it before Benet could take a second helping. There was enough for the Queen, Bella and the Lady, she said as she covered it with a piece of linen.

They had just finished their meal when there was a knock on the door. Thinking it was Bella, 'Liza rushed to open it, a smile on her face.

It was John Serle, his face a picture of anguish as he told them that Ann had gone into labour yester night and was still in the throes. The children were cold and hungry, could Mistress Munnings help? There was no hesitation, and the children were ushered into the warm kitchen and given food and allowed to play ‘Fox and Geese’, although they were not much good at it remarked Benet afterwards.

Bella however, did not appear.

Chapter 30

Ann Serle lived just long enough to hold her mewling son while Midwife Collier baptised him; it was fortunate, Patience Collier told Charity, that she had remembered to renew her baptismal licence before Advent, for the Bishop was a stickler for such licences being kept up to date – not to mention the charges going up each year!

The son, named Stephen after his appearance on that Saint's Day, lived for only a few minutes longer than his mother and his swaddling bands became his shroud. The other children, who had been taken into the Munnings' home late on Christmas Day when Ann's labour was already a day long, came back to the cottage to kiss goodbye to their mother and brother.

As word spread, the room quickly filled with village women, who waited respectfully while Goodwife Sabey and Charity Munnings washed the bodies before wrapping Ann Serle in her shroud and doing the same for the baby whom they laid alongside her, before placing the obligatory taper in the mother's hands.

The pair were then moved to the outside wall under the window and the mourners came in and out, while the children perched on their parents' bed, watching it all with big eyes. They understood their mother had died, but the full import of what that meant for them, in the future, kept them quiet and round-eyed. John

Serle received the condolences with a face which never once betrayed his grief, nor his worry about his young family.

William sent Thomas round with a small pile of logs to keep the place tolerably warm while Charity, 'Liza and Hannah sent food at regular intervals. Until the funeral, there was nothing else to do.

"What John will do with four children to care for, I don't know. I expect Goodwife Sabey will help out, but she can't be there every day," said Charity to Hannah as they sat in the gloom of the firelight, later that evening, supping warmed ale. "Best thing for him is to marry as quickly as possible; I thought young Patience from the Crown, might be suitable. With that queer lip of hers, she can't be choosy," then added, "but now, neither can he."

"Would she take him on with four children?" asked Hannah, wearily, thinking wistfully of the warm bed awaiting her and 'Liza already fast asleep in it.

Charity shrugged. "I'll have a word and see if she's willing. Winter is coming on and that house needs keeping warm, and the family fed if they're to see the Spring. I feel I ought to do something, seeing as how he is a tenant of mine, and Ann was a good soul." She got up, yawned and stretched, banked the fire down and said good night.

Hannah sat for a while longer thinking how unfair life could be – a young mother gone, and husband and children left to survive as best they could. She had been lucky when Johannes had died, she decided, she had a home, a mother to help care for her child and a skill to sell to earn her money to continue to live.

Reverend White was anxious to bury mother and son as quickly as possible and ordered a grave to be dug and the funeral to be held on the Friday, after Holy Innocents' Day. He told John Serle, that, in the circumstances of the sudden death of their mother, he could forgo the usual Innocents' Day whipping of the children in their bed: they had suffered enough.

"Very noble of the Reverend, I'm sure!" said Charity when she heard. She eyed Benet, "You needn't think I will be so generous. If you're going to have a free day from working for me, then you can be whipped and remind yourself of those poor innocent babes murdered by Herod in Bethlehem. They never had the chance to play or go fishing!" and she left him standing sullenly at the kitchen table.

'Liza was fortunate that her mother did not adhere to this particular tradition, so she was able to enjoy her last few moments in bed in peace. The mornings were now cold and dark and despite it still being the festive season, there was still the work to be done on the laundry – icy cold water and furious winds being her usual start to the day.

When the funeral did take place, Hannah cut sprigs of rosemary from the biggest bush in the garden so that each child, as well as 'Liza, could drop them into the grave as a remembrance.

John Serle could not afford a wake for the villagers.

Bella had not attended the funeral but had heard of the tragedy when she called at the house on the last day of the Octave of Christmas – the circumcision of Jesus Christ. Another holy day for the Queen, to be marked by an extra mass and another fast. She was grateful for the suet pie and the chewets she was given to take back with her, which she told them she would share with Lady Darrell; the two of them were learning how to manage the food for themselves.

Richard White had informed them that the Duke of Suffolk was sending two women of his household to help care for the Queen, but Her Majesty refused to allow them to do anything other than fetch and carry her laundry and clean the outer chamber. She told Master White that she had no trust in anyone sent by the Duke. She had also told Father de Athequa that in future she would hear mass in the corridor opposite her rooms. She had no intention of leaving the Tower, so fearful was she of being kidnapped and removed by agents of the King while going to and from the chapel.

"She is so unhappy, and I am too," she shook her head, "obligada a quesarse en un sitio, I am forced to stay solely in one place. Lady Darrell goes in and out to the kitchen and the courtyard, but I have to stay with the Queen when she does; she will not be left on her own. Lady Darrell is with her now. You know, if I could not come and see you, I think I would go mad!" Bella told them. "When I told the Queen that I found it very hard to be inside the Tower all the time, she reminded me of the words of Saint Catherine of Siena, which she said gave her strength and comfort."

"What were those?" asked 'Liza.

"Build a cell inside your mind from which you can never flee. Nothing great is ever achieved without much enduring. Proclaim the truth and do not be silent through fear." Bella recited it with her eyes closed.

Hannah looked at her in surprise. It summed up the attitude of the Queen perfectly but then, the Queen had already endured so much, as well as a lifetime of self-discipline to help her to survive her virtual imprisonment; but not Bella, who was a young girl, yet had been placed in what was effectively a prison and forced to endure much hardship.

"Yesterday, she put her hands around my face and told me, "Necesito que sea mis ojos y mis oidos enel mundo ahora Isabella," it means you must be my eyes and ears on the world now. How can I do this every day for the rest of my life?" Bella gave a half sob and Hannah put her arms around her. She rocked Bella in her arms, much as she would have done a small child, while the girl sobbed and sobbed. Hannah looked at her daughter and glanced towards the chess board.

"Let's have a game of chess – you will have to get your mind in order to beat me, because I beat you last time, remember?" said 'Liza, brightly, and was rewarded by seeing her friend loosen her clutch on her mother's arms, and sit up. Bella nodded and watched 'Liza set out the pieces.

Chapter 31

The Christmas season drew to its usual end on Epiphany, when the wassail cup was passed around and 'Liza hoped that Bella would be able to come and share it with them and relax for a short while. When she did not appear, the well-soaked crust was given to Benet, who ate it eagerly.

The villagers started to prepare for Plough Monday and the resumption of all field work and especially the start of the winter ploughing of the strips in all the fields. The ploughshares were fixed, and the oxen fitted up with their yokes and harnesses in readiness, all of which had given John Serle work to do and brought him some much-needed income.

Charity had wasted no time in sounding out Patience about whether a proposal from John would be welcome. The girl worked hard in the kitchen of the Crown inn, only venturing into the bar when the number of customers increased dramatically. She was extremely conscious of her facial appearance, for her hare lip was pronounced, and she had suffered cruel remarks about it all her life. Nevertheless, she was a kind-hearted, hard-working girl who saw at once, that, marrying John was probably her only chance of escaping from the inn and having a husband and home of her own.

To John, Charity spoke bluntly, he needed a wife to take care of his children and keep home and

Patience would be able to do that, as well as find work with the laundry too, just as Ann had done before. She said he knew that Patience was a good girl and added, that, in the dark the hare lip would not be noticeable! Charity then quite deliberately stopped helping him with the children and the cooking and told Goodwife Sabey to do the same.

By the end of the week following Christmas, John Serle realised that he could not hope to work as he had been doing with no one at home to look after the children. He genuinely grieved for Ann, whom he had dearly loved, but realised that marrying Patience was the only solution to his present difficulties.

Accordingly, he asked Charity to invite Patience to the laundry after church and in front of Hannah, 'Liza and Mistress Munnings asked Patience if she would become his wife. He warned her that the children were difficult, and the cottage was a mess, and that while he did not love her, he would honour her.

It was as much as Patience could hope for, and she said yes immediately. As her parents were dead, she asked Charity to come with them both as they trooped out of the house to speak with the vicar, and, as a result of Charity's persistence, which she told the vicar was due to her concern for both John and the children, the date for the wedding was agreed.

How it would all turn out, was anyone's guess, but on the following Friday, they were married in the church porch in front of many villagers and Patience left the inn to begin her new life in the cottage.

January was a bitterly cold month and frost and ice formed instantly on all exposed surfaces. Bella sent word that the Queen was unwell, with a bad cough and chills and that she required constant care from her and Lady Darrell, thus it would be difficult for her to come and see them.

In spite of wearing two pairs of woollen stockings and two shifts, as well as her thickest woollen overdress, two shawls, and a pair of mittens, 'Liza found working outside to be beyond her. She was driven into the kitchen many times during the day to warm herself for a short while before returning to the laundry. Benet too was suffering because he had started to cough at night and said he felt sick when out in the cold air. Both Hannah and Charity feared that he was weakening and what was even more worrying was that the winter had barely started.

'Liza looked at the sky anxiously on St Paul's Day, for at breakfast Benet had repeated the old saying, "If St Paul's day be fair and clear, it doth betide a happy year". 'Liza wanted there to be some happiness for them all, not least for Bella, stuck in the Tower with a sick woman and no relief from the prayers and services that were the only things that filled the day.

The day remained overcast.

That very same day, Bella was watching from one of the Tower windows as the starlings wheeled across the sky, soaring and diving like a huge moving cloud of smoke; she wondered what such freedom must feel like. She sighed and wrapped her shawl more tightly around her for it was cold on the gallery where the wind whistled its way into the Tower. The second mass of the day was over, and she was clearing everything from the gallery, as she always did; a daily chore and the prie-de-dieu still had to be taken back into the bedchamber.

Kitchen Agnes had just come up with a basket of food and told her that the two Suffolk women were complaining again to Mistress Fauconer, about Lady Darrell and the Queen treating them like under servants rather than the ladies they were. However, she said triumphantly, the housekeeper had given them short shrift, saying that their positions and work were nothing to do with her, and they should voice their dissatisfaction to their Duke or to the steward. "That told them" Agnes said gleefully before departing to the warmth of her kitchen.

Sighing, Bella wandered back into the outer chamber and put the basket down before returning to the gallery. She would have liked to go to see 'Liza and maybe have a game of chess or 'Fox and Goose' with Benet, despite the smoke and lingering smell of food there, for the kitchen would be warm with conversation and laughter, and she would feel their care for her, and be happy for a part of the day.

The Queen reminded her that it was the Feast of the Purification of the Blessed Virgin and they would be fasting until the first Mass of the day on the morrow. Bella was heartily sick of her life at the moment, and even the passing of messages had become a routine event to her. She no longer felt a thrill when she handed one over, or, received one from ‘Liza.

Chapter 32

Candlemass had come – it was an important day in the life of the church, with candles lit in all the homes and all over the church; as well as everyone carrying an additional taper when they attended Mass. The chandler had been busy! In accordance with ancient practice, Charity and the other housewives had put a sprig of rowan over the front and back doors and Benet was now disposing of all the Christmas greenery, on the fire, where it curled and flamed while the berries spat as they shrivelled and died.

While he did this he chanted "If Candelmass be fair and bright, come winter have another flight. If Candlemass brings cloud and rain, go winter and come not here again" over and over until 'Liza shouted at him to stop.

"It's a bright, cloudless day Benet and you saying that over and over won't change things. Just accept it". She was irritable and angry for she suspected that she had chilblains on her heels, and they itched and burned in equal measure.

Benet went quiet as instructed and then started coughing and coughing and coughing. Hannah took him over to the corner and made him sit down while she fetched his mother's rose hip mixture for him to sip. Privately she wondered if she might presume on her service to the Queen and ask if one of her apothecaries could give them something more powerful for him.

Patience Serle, who had been helping out with the laundry, had already taken some of the syrup for her youngest stepchild, but had pretended not to hear 'Liza, when she had asked her how things were at the cottage. She was not looking her best, thought 'Liza, pale face and black-ringed eyes which might just be because of the disturbed nights she was having. 'Liza hoped it was nothing more serious.

As February eased into the year, the lambing began in earnest and John Serle spent more and more time in the fields helping out, he found it a great relief to be away from his sick and sad children and a wife who rarely spoke. Working on the strips with his neighbours allowed him to forget how miserable he was.

He was returning home in the dusk of the day, thinking about nothing in particular when he noticed a group of youths near Hogsherd Close; there was some shouting and scuffling and he plainly heard Benet Munnings shouting, "Give it b b back!"

Running up the roadway he was in time to see three of the Shelley boys and their followers tossing a willow basket from one to another and jeering at Benet, who was too short to intercept it. John Serle elbowed two boys out of the way and caught the basket just as the lid flew open and a tiny kitten fell onto the ground.

Benet swooped down and picked it up, cradling it against his chest, while the animal whimpered and mewled; the boys took to their heels and disappeared into the gloom of the evening leaving the man and Benet to sort themselves out.

Benet was crying as he snuggled the kitten into his chest for warmth and told John Serle how he had seen the gang of youths drowning kittens, one after the other, laughing as they did so. The bedraggled black and white bundle in his arms was the only survivor and Benet had sneaked forward to rescue it from the sack on the ground and put it into his basket. Unfortunately, the others had noticed him and given chase, snatching the basket and using it as a ball. The man walked alongside him until he reached the laundry and told him he would have to learn how to fight, or he would always lose out to the village lads.

Benet adored kittens. He was devastated when his mother told him that he would have to find someone else to look after it, they had enough cats. Benet who was encouraging the kitten to lap some milk at the time, shook his head, but Charity was adamant. "I want it gone by the time I come back from William's," she told him.

'Liza found him still whispering to and cuddling the kitten when she came in from the yard and asked him where he had found it. Benet recounted the saga, adding that his mother had demanded that the kitten be thrown out of the house. The other cats weren't interested in it he told her sorrowfully, in fact some of them had hissed at it.

'Liza looked at his woebegone face and had a bright idea, "What about Bella?" she asked, "maybe she could look after it?"

There and then he insisted that they go to the Palace and see her. It was quite dark by now and 'Liza was not very happy about disturbing the guards and the household, but on seeing his distress, she agreed to go with him to the Tower and speak to Lady Darrell. The matter of getting past the guards was easily solved with a trolley whose leather top both covered the basket and kept the lid on the kitten.

Although Lady Darrell was not too happy about the suggestion that Bella have a pet kitten, after seeing the girl talking to and cuddling the reluctant animal, her face happy for once, she changed her mind. She would talk to Her Majesty about it she promised, but Bella would be in sole charge and if anything went wrong the kitten would have to go. Bella promised that she would be the best carer ever, and while they waited for Lady Darrell to return, 'Liza had a few words with her friend.

The kitten had already brightened Bella's day and she was at risk of smothering it to death with her cuddling; 'Liza told her to make sure that it could not get out and that she must remind Kitchen Agnes to bring up some milk. There was no message to be delivered and no need to stay after Lady Darrell brought word that the Queen had given permission for Bella to keep the animal - for now.

Bella allowed Benet to kiss it goodbye then ran back up the staircase, and even forgot to say goodbye to her friend.

Lady Darrell straightened the leather cover and said, "You need to go home quickly, and keep safe, for the weather is inclement and the guards will change soon." A hint that they should be careful, thought 'Liza, who began to walk back with Benet. She found the message tucked under the basket lid and safely transferred it to Hannah's workbasket containing the pieces of linen collar without anyone noticing, telling her mother later when they were in bed.

That night, as she lay in bed, listening to the wind moan and the thatch creak, 'Liza wondered if the message was for the Princess Mary whose birthday occurred on the following Sunday, according to Bella. How awful not to be able to see your mother on your birthday, she thought. There were times she resented the strict control that her own mother exerted over her, but she knew it would always be for the best. Her Mami loved her.

Days passed, and after the Shrove Tuesday football game was played, they all trooped home to get warm and unexpectedly found Bella sheltering under the outhut waiting for them, the kitten with her, partly to allow Benet to play with it, but mainly to keep it out of mischief while she was away from the chamber, for its sharp teeth and claws had already damaged several parts of the tapestry and it had pulled the table runner off the table more than once. She had no idea whether or not it was a boy or girl but had named it 'Benedetta' after Benet. He was very pleased at this.

"Lent starts tomorrow and so the Queen will fast again. She is not well but will not take Doctor de la Sa's advice to eat a little each day to keep her strength up. What can we do?" She wrapped her arms around her body and rocked to and fro.

"It has been wearisome for her, for us all." She looked at 'Liza, "I find it more and more difficult to get her permission to leave the Tower and come here to see you. If it were not for, er, our arrangement, I think she would stop me coming altogether."

'Liza nodded. "Mami wants it all to stop anyway, she thinks the risk is too great, and especially with all the rumours in the village about what the King is going to do," she smiled at her friend, shaking her head free from such worrying thoughts, "Come on, Mami made some jumbles this morning, and then we'll have a game of chess!"

Chapter 33

Edward Swarthye visited them briefly, shortly before Easter; he warned them that all the rumours swirling round the London inns and tap rooms, were bad news for Katharine and her supporters. The new Queen, Anne, was a champion of the Church Reformers and had the King's ear – and the Catholic Church was suffering on all sides. His parting words were that Hannah might not be required to send the embroidered collars for much longer. He would let her know as soon as he could, but he did not say why the arrangement would stop.

A travelling chapman brought news that the Pope had declared Katharine's marriage to Henry as both valid and canonical. It was a decision that had further angered the King, although it instantly lifted the mood of Queen Katharine and her two faithful companions, prompting the Queen to write an open letter to the Spanish Ambassador immediately, which the Steward was reluctantly forced to send.

However, the next news to arrive with the pedlars was not good, for the King had managed to get Parliament to finally pass the Act of Succession, and not only was Princess Mary barred from the accession in favour of her half-sister, but it was also now treason to call Katharine, or even refer to her, as 'Queen'. The news also brought a flurry of messages with John Carter to be smuggled into the Queen, so that 'Liza wondered if there was some sort of plan to rescue the Queen. She said as much when she next saw Bella.

"She would never leave this land while her daughter is here and under threat," Bella told her; she was eating some bread and honey which meant she had broken her fast yet again, but it had cheered her up and she was willing to confess her sin to Father de Athequa, who understood how difficult her life was, and treated her gently.

The gradual loosening of winter's grip, and longer daylight, lifted everyone's spirits, but it remained a cold Spring, and people in the village looked forward to summer again. Food was becoming more difficult to find, for the turnips were soft, and the beans had gone black. The dried pork had long since finished and the barley broth was monotonous, even though Hannah did her best to flavour it with herbs, onion and bacon.

In the little cottage, Patience Serle was forced to make acorn bread, and pea and barley mash with carrot, day after day, until the children cried and refused to eat it again. She often wished she had never been persuaded to marry John Serle, for at least at the inn she had been well fed and chatted to the other servants all the time she was working. Even more importantly she could sleep undisturbed each night; but here, the children were often sick and poorly and night-times were the worst. Her husband came home each night, weary and capable only of eating his supper before falling into a deep sleep, with barely a word for his wife. With the children unhappy and restless and little support from her husband, Patience Serle felt as if the whole world was settled on her shoulders.

On hearing that the Act of Succession was now law – a fact quite literally shouted in the streets of the village, a group of villagers led by Michael, staged a silent demonstration in support of the Queen. The guards were angry and suspicious, and the steward begged them to go home; but it was not until Lady Darrell came out to them with a message from the Queen, thanking them for their loyalty but telling them to return home and take no hurt on her behalf, that the villagers left. Things were getting quite tense.

Looking back later, 'Liza could see that in some ways life seemed to speed up after Easter. They went to church of course, in Holy Week, and on Maundy Thursday, she accompanied Charity as they were told to wash the altars with water and wine under the supervision of the churchwarden. Bella had told them that the Queen was observing 'Semanca' - Holy Week – with a fervour which showed how worried she was about her own future.

Watching the vicar on his knees creeping to the Cross in the dark church on Easter Sunday morning while the bells tolled mournfully only reinforced 'Liza's vague feeling that something bad was going to happen to one or all of them very soon, and even after she lit her candle from the brazier at the chancel steps and kissed the crucifix held by Reverend White, she felt her depression deepen.

As usual, all those around her were happy and carefree as the Sepulchre was opened and the church lit up with candle after candle, but 'Liza did not find her own mood lighten and feeling downhearted, she elected to go for a walk by herself that afternoon, rather than join the Gilbert family as they celebrated Easter.

She returned in time to see Benet talking to one of the grooms who was hanging about the house: Bella had been forced to send a sad message, the kitten now larger and more playful than ever, had to go from the Tower. The Queen had found her best velvet slippers had been extensively chewed and lost her temper. 'Liza took a basket from the kitchen cupboard and told Benet she would bring it safely back. Meanwhile, she suggested his aunt might be in need of a mouser and immediately he vanished back up the road to the Gilbert's house, for he was sure that his aunt would find a home for the orphan.

It was the first time the two girls had walked in the park for months and they were amazed at the sight of the primroses and bluebells which covered the ground beneath the trees. The blackthorn was in full blossom, its heady scent almost overpowering them when they perched on a dry patch of grass. They were met on the path by John Serle who had been sent in search of a large swarm of bees which had suddenly taken off from the beehives in the wood over the road.

After he had gone, ‘Liza told Bella that the villagers believed that a swarming meant someone in the area would be leaving, and she hoped it did not mean the Queen, or her new friend; but seeing Bella’s face she decided not to also tell her how shaken she had felt on Easter Sunday.

Bella, already upset at losing the kitten now burst into tears. She was worn down with the constraints of living in the Tower, living with the Queen who was becoming more and more pious and withdrawn from life, which had repercussions for her women; not that serving God was wrong, she hastily told ’Liza, but it was very monotonous.

No one laughed or smiled any longer, also the Queen had a terrible cough and the doctor seemed unable to treat it, so their nights were disturbed even when the Queen was sleeping.

She heaved a sigh, “I never go anywhere, I am not even allowed to see you, for the door is only unlocked for cleaning or fetching food, and those Suffolk women! You wouldn’t believe their snide comments as they come and go in the chamber, and all we can do is pretend we don’t hear them.” More tears followed, for Bella felt her life was slipping away, and that no one cared about what was happening to her, and she resented that.

‘Lisa was at a loss to know what to say in reply, so she patted Bella’s knee, “Don’t worry, the villagers won’t let anything happen to the Queen or you. We’ll be watching for the Duke and his henchmen and they won't take you away!"

Bella wished she could believe her, but she had had a terrible feeling for days, that something awful was going to happen. She wiped the last tears from her face and looked around her. The smell of the blackthorn blossom was making her head swim and, she told 'Liza, she was suffering from a ringing in her ears.

Thinking that she would make her friend laugh as she had in the past, 'Liza told her that she had better start praying more, for the ringing was a sign that the souls in Purgatory were calling for her prayers. That information had the opposite effect, however, and made Bella shiver and become even more fearful. She sprang to her feet, reminding 'Liza that on their return, she should retrieve the kitten from the cupboard in the outer room, where the Queen had demanded it be kept until it could be taken away.

Chapter 34

Had she but known it, this was the last time, she would see Bella. 'Liza had no idea that when they said good-bye to each other then, that it was a farewell forever in truth; for less than a week later a small number of men arrived at the gatehouse, trotting up the street early in the morning, with no fanfare, but ominously with a couple of empty horse litters in their midst. They had come from Kimbolton Castle.

It seems that Thomas Cromwell had learned from the last attempt to remove Katharine of Aragon from Bugden Tower; the tower door was unlocked at the beginning of the day, to allow the servants access to clean the Queen's accommodation and the Queen herself was in the gallery getting ready for Mass. It took just a few minutes to bundle her down the stairs and into one of the litters, where two of Lord Bedingfields's serving women were waiting for her, supposedly to help her on the journey, but actually, to prevent her leaving the litter. The chamberlain at Kimbolton had received specific instructions about how to remove the Queen from Bugden Palace.

Bella and Lady Darrell were just as swiftly put into the second litter, and they were out of the village, and on their way to Kimbolton Castle before any of the villagers could organise themselves. The few that realised what was happening, stood silently, removing their hats and staring forlornly at the small group as they passed.

The remaining household servants followed a short time later, leaving the Suffolk women to pack up the Queen's belongings.

Just like that – they were gone.

Of course, life in the village continued at its normal pace and what had happened to the Queen that morning was talked about until, with time, even that stopped. Sometimes, at night, 'Liza and her mother whispered together about the time they had been a part of some dangerous network of supporters of the Queen, but the linen collars were no longer required – Edward had written to them the week after Queen Katharine left Bugden and when he visited them in early summer, he told them it was best not to ask him any further questions about any of it.

Hannah accepted the change in her fortunes without further comment, but she began to mentally tot up the amount of money she had managed to save, and to wonder if John Carter might give them a special rate to travel to London. Perhaps, she would have enough, but it would be best not to mention her plan returning to London until she had spoken with Edward on his next visit in the autumn, for there would be accommodation to arrange and work to be solicited - in the city.

Life took on its daily routine.

Part way through the morning's work, 'Liza needed to go to the privy, and unwillingly picked up the bucket of food waste and kitchen slops; it was really Benet's job to feed the pigs, but he had either forgotten or deliberately left it for her to do.

Mistress Munnings merely looked at her face and pursed her lips, "If you are on your way to the privy as you just said, then it is hardly out of your way to take the slops to the pigs," she paused, "and don't be long! I need you to help me with these sheets from the Crown."

The privy was sited next to but a little higher than, the pigpen, with the waste shute over a wooden trough, although the large eating trough was handily near the gate and she poured the bucket's contents straight into it, as the two sows came trundling and snorting over to feed, followed by their half-grown piglets, squeaking and jostling each other as they did so.

She entered the privy, and shut the lower door behind her, leaving the top undone since she had seen Benet leave with one of the hand carts to collect more dirty laundry from the inns. It seemed safe enough with Benet out of the way, and the place stinking already in the warmth of the day. She was heartily sick of the game he liked to play of trying to see her with her skirts up.

She settled herself, and thought about the latest village gossip, and wondered fleetingly how Bella was, and what she was doing this day. She had hoped that Bella would have been able to get a message to her, but so far, there was only silence. Was the Queen well she wondered? They heard only now and then from the pedlars about her life at Kimbolton and it seemed she was rarely to be seen.

She finished and dipped the moss stick into the bucket to wipe herself. She could already hear the pigs snuffling as they ate her waste. Disgusting really, to eat that! She wondered again if that was why her mother never ate pork. 'Liza was not so fussy – so long as she didn't stop to think about what the pigs ate.

Descending the wooden steps outside, she realised that Benet had already cut the lye soap blocks for her, and there was nothing now to stop her from getting on with the washing. Stepping out of her clogs, she hitched up her skirts, tucking them into the apron ties, and tipped the first basket of laundry and the soap into the tub.

Then she began the methodical stamping up and down, while in her head she sang one of the Spanish songs that her grandmother used to sing to her when she was small.

GLOSSARY

Chewets	Small meat pies with a crinkle top
Crumpsey	Peaky, sickly
Dauncey	Peaky, ill looking
Dot and go	Someone walking very unevenly
Garderobe	Toilet, so called because it was believed that the bad smell kept the moths away and the clothes free of holes
Halberd	A long shafted axe-like weapon
Hippocras	Sweet wine
Hoydens	Tomboys/loud behaviour
Jag	Small bundle of straw or hay
Jakes	Toilet
Jumbles	Biscuits
Knickled	Flattened (as in a crop)
Lawn	Very fine and expensive linen

Peggles	Cowslips
Razzled meat	Meat cooked black on the outside but still raw on the inside
Shawn	A type of oboe
Shofar	Jewish trumpet made from a ram's horn
Skep(s)	Beehives(s)
Soul cake	Small cake baked on All Hallow's Eve and given to visitors in return for their prayers for the soul of the giver
Stultch	A vertical strip of bound straw thatch for roofing
Shet knife	Pocket or folding knife
Slummock(y)	Messy, untidy
Tippett	Band of fur or cloth decorating a sleeve
Twattle	Gossip

Wemble	Inverting a pot or pan to keep the inside clean
Yerm	One bundle of staw for thatching

SPANISH

(Los) plebeyo(s)	Common people, commoner(s)
(El) jabon de Castile	Castile soap
Ella desunocia el monde	She does not know (knows nothing) of the world
Libre como el viento	Free as the wind (free as a bird)
Entiende?	Understand?
Os le mantendre en mis oraciones cada noche	I will keep you (all) in my prayers each night
Necesito que sea mis ojos y mis oidos ene	You must be my eyes and ears on

Mudo ahora, Isabella	The world now, Isabella

Quarter Days for payment of rent, dues and for Hiring of servants etc	25 March, 24 June, 29 September, 25 December

Julian calendar was used in Tudor times – we use the Gregorian calendar, which was adopted in 1582, and resulted in the 'loss' of 11 days. All dates given are modern dates.

Money	A crown was worth £110.32 today. Shilling = £22 today and 5 shillings was 8 days' pay for a skilled craftsman Groat = £3.60. 1£ = 240 pennies and 1 penny = £1.50
Catherine of Siena	1347 – 1380. Lay member of the Dominican Order who was considered a mystic and canonised for her work among the poor and needy.

Rosh Hashannah	Jewish festival celebrating God's creation of the world. The Jewish New Year, calculated from the new moon nearest the autumn equinox, sometime in September through October. The shofar is blown at this feast.
Divine office – daily	Matins (2/3 am) Lauds (5 am) Prime (6 am) Tierce (9am) Sext (noon) Nones (3 pm or 9 hours from sunrise) Vespers (6 pm) Compline (7 pm or just before bed 8-9 pm) Used to tell the time for the villagers

AFTERWORD

The events I have included in this novel are based on the known facts of the Queen's ten months' incarceration at Buckden Palace from July 1533 to May 1534, which happened during Henry Eighth's "Great Matter" that is, his divorce from Katharine of Aragon. The Queen was moved several times as the divorce dragged on, the latest move being from Ampthill to Buckden, and the last move to Kimbolton, where she died in 1536. She is buried in Peterborough Cathedral.

In Tudor England, women of all classes were brought up to believe that they were inferior to men in every way, including the size of their brains!! and they enjoyed few legal rights in their own name.

In addition, the Roman Catholic Church – England's religion at that time, taught that women were the cause of mankind's Original Sin, for which Jesus Christ was crucified in atonement, and all women were by default sinful. Therefore, in any dispute, they were assumed to be at fault/wrong/ guilty.

Any independence of thought, behaviour or belief was barred by the father or the husband or the brother if they lived in his household; and it was generally held that education was wasted on women. The only exceptions to this, being the daughters, and therefore future wives of monarchs and noblemen who were expected to read and write and be able to take part in state occasions, and who were to be taught to be godly and moral and set a good example to those beneath them. They were not thought to be capable of brave or independent action.

Of course, there were exceptions to this, and Sir Thomas More is one of the finest examples at this time, for he educated his daughters along with his sons; also there were several wives of guildsmen and tradesmen who helped to run their husbands' businesses. However, this was not a norm for society, especially in the countryside.

Dates are tricky for this period – the dates I have used follow the Gregorian calendar that we use today. It was adopted in 1582 when 11 days were 'lost' from the old Julian calendar; there is therefore sometimes a disparity in dates given in reference books, depending on which calendar has been followed.

LINDA UPHAM

Born in Yorkshire, and an only child, I developed an early passion for both reading and history.

A history graduate and retired teacher I hope to bring history alive to children through my novels.

My first children's novel, The Bronze Dagger, for 9 to 14 year olds, was set in Roman times and featured a girl as the main character (as do all my books). My second, Divided Loyalties, is set in the period following the Norman Conquest and again, featured our local area around Huntingdon. Discord again is set in Huntingdon during the Civil War. This book, Intrigue at Buckden Towers, is set in my local village Buckden and during the Tudor times of Henry VIII and Queen Katherine of Aragon.

I have one other book published, especially for my grandsons, titled Grandma's Bedtime Stories.

Bronze Dagger - ISBN 0-7188-2775-9
Divided Loyalties - ISBN 978-0755203-02-4
Discord - ISBN 978-1-80369-251-7

Grandma's Bedtime Stories ISBN 978-1-80369-099-5

Lightning Source UK Ltd.
Milton Keynes UK
UKHW021026171222
414087UK00010B/358